TRUE CONFESSIONS

Visit us at www.boldstrokesbooks.com

Praise for *From This Moment On*

"The story of two women faced with crushing loss…who find something to love again. A fine read for coping with loss as well as being a touching lesbian romance."—*Midwest Book Review*

"Trebelhorn created characters for *From This Moment On* that are flawed, faulted, and wholly realistic. While many of the characters are struggling with loss, their unique approaches to dealing with it reveal their weaknesses and give the reader a deeper appreciation of the characters.…*From This Moment On*…tells a gripping, emotional story about love, loss, and the fusion of the two."—*Philadelphia Gay News*

By the Author

From This Moment On

True Confessions

TRUE CONFESSIONS

by

PJ Trebelhorn

2011

TRUE CONFESSIONS

ISBN 10: 1-60282-216-6
ISBN 13: 978-1-60282-216-0

THIS TRADE PAPERBACK ORIGINAL IS PUBLISHED BY
BOLD STROKES BOOKS, INC.
P.O. BOX 249
VALLEY FALLS, NY 12185

FIRST EDITION: APRIL 2011

CREDITS
EDITOR: VICTORIA OLDHAM AND SHELLEY THRASHER
PRODUCTION DESIGN: STACIA SEAMAN
COVER DESIGN BY SHERI (GRAPHICARTIST2020@HOTMAIL.COM)

Acknowledgments

This book has been a long time coming, and I want to thank Len Barot and Bold Strokes Books for giving me the opportunity to finally see it published. I truly am blessed to be a part of the BSB family.

To my beta readers Nikki G. and Cathy R.—your help was invaluable in shaping this one up. I cannot thank you enough.

To my editor, Victoria Oldham—I thank you for once again helping me through the process of making this a better book. And to Shelley Thrasher, your help was also very much appreciated, and I know your words of wisdom will help me in future works.

To cover artist Sheri—wow. I really don't know what to say about your work that hasn't been said already. You are truly amazing.

Dedication

For Cheryl,
because you continue to support me in this madness.
I can't even begin to tell you how much you mean to me.

CHAPTER ONE

L ynn Patrick glanced at the calendar. She'd been trying to write for the past four hours because her next novel was due for edits in eight weeks. But all she could think about was leaving San Francisco the next morning to drive six hundred plus miles to Portland for three weeks of December. She made the trip every year to her hometown to celebrate her parents' anniversary, her younger brother's birthday, and Christmas. And every year before that trip, she suffered these same anxiety attacks. They had nothing to do with her family and absolutely everything to do with Jessica Greenfield.

Despite the miles that separated them, Lynn and Jessie managed to keep in touch through phone calls and e-mails. They were still best friends, as they had been since second grade. Even Lynn moving away from home right after high school hadn't changed that fact. It had been her dream to go to Hollywood and become a screenwriter, but when she made it as far as San Francisco she fell in love with the city and never left. After a few years of trying to sell her screenplays, she finally decided to try writing novels. She'd become successful, but not rich. Eventually she'd accepted that she'd never have a *New York Times* bestseller as a lesbian romance novelist.

Sometime during the next weeks she and Jessie would spend time together, and this year, like every year, Lynn considered telling Jessie she loved her. But every year Jessie's husband and six-year-old daughter, Amber, kept Lynn from saying a word about it. She shook her head at her fantasy. Jessie was straight and had a family.

Lynn would never actually tell Jessie how she felt, but she kept on dreaming about what might be.

Lynn sighed and stretched back in her chair, trying to relax. Oscar, her very aloof feline companion, gave a bored yawn from his hammock-style window seat a few feet away. The gorgeous view of the Golden Gate Bridge was wasted on the cat, but he loved sitting in that window. Luckily, with the open loft, the view was exquisite from every window.

"Oh, please. Like your life is any more exciting than mine." She tossed her pen on the desk then headed to the kitchen for some wine. Glass in hand, she'd just settled into the couch when the phone rang.

"Hey, big sister."

Lynn grinned at her brother Charlie's greeting. He liked to make it sound as if she were ancient, when she was actually only thirty-three, a year older than he was. They'd always been close, and Charlie calmed her nerves. He'd been her rock for most of her adult life.

"What's up, Chuck?" Lynn laughed while he groaned in response to the tired old line.

"Jesus, what are we, twelve?" He laughed too, but Lynn knew he hated the nickname—which is exactly why she continued to use it. "I have some news for you, and I really think I should get something in return."

"It's that big, huh?" She put her feet up on the coffee table and lifted her arm as Oscar pushed his way onto her lap, his motor running loudly.

"The biggest. What's your best offer?"

"I'll be civil to your witch of a wife for the holidays." Lynn sipped her wine and shuddered. Charlie's wife *hated* her and wouldn't let Lynn anywhere near their kids. She seemed convinced that Lynn was some kind of recruiter for homosexuals, as though her sexual preference was infectious and her kids would catch lesbian cooties. "On second thought, I rescind that offer."

"No need, since she won't be around anyway. She finally decided to take the kids and move back home to her mother."

Lynn almost spat her wine all over herself and Oscar. She bent to place her glass on the table and Oscar jumped down, tossing her a dirty look over his shoulder while he sauntered away, swishing his gray tail.

"*She* left *you*? Holy crap, that *is* big news."

"Believe it or not, that isn't the news I'm calling about. We can talk about my marital woes over a few drinks while you're in town."

"Deal. So tell me what you did call for, because if it's not that, it must be *really* big."

"I ran into Jessie Greenfield at the supermarket this afternoon. Have you talked to her lately?"

"Why? What's going on?" Lynn quickly lost her patience when it came to news about Jessie. "Is she all right?"

"Her husband left about a week ago to work some construction job in Las Vegas. He'll be gone until after the first of the year."

"He's an architect, Charlie. Sometimes he goes to a site to troubleshoot problems with a design. What's so big about that?"

"I got the distinct impression this is more than a simple job away from home." He paused, obviously waiting for her to say something. She managed to resist, if only to irritate the hell out of him. "I think they've separated."

Lynn's heart stuttered and she clutched the phone tighter. She closed her eyes. For the past eight years she'd dreamt of the day Jessie finally woke up and realized what an ass Wayne was.

"She actually told you that?" They'd lived across the street from Jessie's family for years, and while they'd all been fairly close, she couldn't envision Jessie sharing that kind of information with Charlie. Especially since Jessie probably would have told her about something that big herself.

"Well, not exactly," he admitted. "She said he wouldn't be here for Christmas, and I made some remark about how it must be really rough to be apart for the holidays. She just shrugged and didn't say anything else about it."

"And from that brief conversation you concluded that they separated? Charlie, you must be a genius. Should I call Mensa?"

Lynn laughed, but he grumbled something on the other end of the line. "What was that? I missed what you said."

"I said you're a bitch." She would have thought he meant it if he hadn't started laughing. "You can make fun of me all you want, but you wait. I'll bet you twenty bucks they're separated. In fact, I'll bet you *fifty* that they're headed for divorce."

Lynn heard a knock and glanced at the front door. "I'm not about to bet on the state of Jessie's marriage. I've got to go. See you tomorrow."

"What time are you getting here?"

"I'm leaving first thing in the morning, so hopefully I'll get there around dinnertime."

They said their good-byes, and Lynn hung up as she opened the door.

Shit.

"You forgot," Bri said without emotion, and with only a cursory glance at Lynn. She walked in without being invited and headed straight for the kitchen, most probably to get herself a glass of wine. "I guess I shouldn't be surprised, really. You always seem to forget when we've planned to go out to the bar. Even when we talked about it a few hours ago."

"I didn't forget," Lynn lied. She shut the door and returned to her seat on the couch. Lynn looked down at her clothes—jeans with holes where the knees should be and an ancient Portland Winterhawks T-shirt, but she loved her hometown junior hockey team. She held the phone out to Bri in a weak attempt to explain herself. "I was just about to call you. I really don't feel like doing the bar scene tonight."

Bri cocked her head to the side and tried to touch her forehead, but Lynn backed away.

"I don't believe you were going to call me, but something else troubles me more. Are you sick?" Bri asked sincerely. "Since when does Lynn Patrick not feel like hanging out in the bars? I believe you once told me how you love the variety of women here in San Francisco. Perhaps you're getting too old to keep up with the demands all of these women make on your time."

"Bite your tongue." Lynn gasped in mock horror.

"Maybe you should have stayed with Mandy instead of dumping her for someone hotter. You'd have gotten some sleep, anyway."

"But I wouldn't have had as much fun," Lynn said, and grinned. The blind date Bri had set her up with the night before had been turning into a monotonous exercise until the bartender had passed Lynn her phone number. The boring date was gone in a flash, and the bartender had made good on her promise to show Lynn a good time. All night. "That's not why I don't want to go. I've got a hell of a long drive tomorrow. I'm leaving first thing in the morning for Portland."

"It's still early." Bri looked at her watch to emphasize that it was only six. "Nobody says you have to close the bar, dear. How much did you write today?"

"I don't know, maybe two words?" Bri laughed. Lynn supported herself well as a freelance copywriter—composing advertising letters for various companies. She spent whatever time was left writing her novels. The manuscript she was working on was due by the end of January, and her editor would be pissed because she wasn't getting anywhere with it. She would probably end up working more during the trip home than she'd originally planned.

Lynn stretched out her legs on the coffee table and studied Bri as she settled in and took a sip of her wine. Bri's blond hair glowed next to Lynn's black mane, and although only an inch shorter than Lynn, she was also seven years older. Bri was striking in an elegant sort of way, and Lynn had been attracted to her from the moment they met at the animal shelter—the day Lynn adopted Oscar and Bri adopted a dog for her mother. Their sexual relationship had lasted only a few months three years earlier, but they remained good friends.

Bri, a psychologist, had plenty to say about Lynn's unrequited love for Jessica Greenfield. According to Bri, Lynn's feelings for Jessie made it impossible for Lynn to have any kind of long-term relationship. But it had nothing to do with Jessie. Lynn had convinced herself over the years that she would have more fun single than she could ever have in a relationship.

"You cut your hair." Lynn's tone was casual. "Short looks really good on you, Bri."

"Thank you." Bri glanced at Lynn before shifting on the couch in order to face her. She ran her fingers through the back of Lynn's hair once. "And yours looks better since you've decided to let it grow to your shoulders. With a purse, some makeup, and a new pair of shoes, you could actually pass as a straight girl."

"Plenty of straight women don't carry a purse *or* wear makeup. And I don't need those things to pass as straight. My share of men ask me out." Lynn smiled at her. "I also don't need twenty-seven pairs of shoes in my closet. Besides that, I don't want to be a femme."

"It wouldn't hurt you to wear something other than tennis shoes, you know." Bri gave her a playful shove on the arm. "Frankly, I'm surprised you even noticed that I cut my hair. You aren't usually very observant of things like that. You remind me of my ex-husband that way."

"Ouch." Lynn winced and placed her hand over her heart as she looked at Bri. "Am I really that bad?"

"Sometimes—but you have your moments." Bri gave her a quick once-over, shaking her head. "Go change so we can get there early."

"I'm not going."

"I've never known you to pass up a wet T-shirt contest before." Bri smiled slightly. "What's going on with you?"

"I'm thinking it would be unwise to drive six hundred miles with a hangover. I'm tired, Bri. Nothing's *going on* with me." Lynn put her feet on the floor and placed her elbows on her knees. "You're watching Oscar for me, right?"

"That cat hates me."

"He doesn't *hate* you." Lynn laughed at Bri's look of apprehension. "He just hasn't warmed up to you yet."

"Warmed up to me?" Bri sounded incredulous. "You've had him for almost three years, Lynn. Christ, I was even there the day you picked him out at the shelter. And he still hisses at me when I try to pet him."

"He picked me," Lynn said, with an affectionate glance in

Oscar's direction. "Besides, you know where his food is, and you already have a key to the loft. I'll be back by New Year's Eve."

Lynn finished her wine and watched Bri, who was shaking her head. Bri would take care of Oscar, she always did. Despite her protests, Bri cared about him almost as much as Lynn did. But there was only one way to get her to agree. With a sigh, Lynn finally gave in.

"Okay," she said. "I'll go with you tonight if you'll tend to him."

"And enter the contest?"

"Don't push your luck."

"You could win."

"Probably." Lynn nodded, and Bri slapped her good-naturedly on the thigh. "But come on—what fun would it be to let everyone see my tits?"

"What difference does it make? They've all seen them anyway."

"Wow. You sound a tad jealous, Ms. Cabot. Just because I get lucky once in a while—"

"Once in a while, my ass." Bri guffawed. "My God, Lynn, you could walk into that bar and within ten minutes be on your way home with some woman. What irks me the most is that you know it. You could bring home a different woman every night of the week without even thinking about it."

"But I don't, do I? Despite what everyone thinks of me, I'm not a player. But I sure as hell could be, based on the local sales of my books. I refuse to use my fame to help me pick up a woman, though. You know as well as I do that I don't *need* my status as a hot author to get a woman."

Lynn attempted to stand so she could get more wine, but Bri grabbed her forearm and pulled her back down. Lynn was more surprised than anything, but refused to let it show. Bri's grip didn't lessen. "You are jealous, aren't you, Bri?"

"You're lucky I know you're not as cocky as you'd like people to believe," Bri said. "I'm about to give you a bit of advice."

"Are you going to charge me for this impromptu session?"

"I couldn't be your therapist now, even if I wanted to. You should feel privileged that I don't make you pay." Bri finally loosened her hold on Lynn's arm. "You may not believe this, Lynn, but it really doesn't bother me to see you with other women. I know you and I are friends, and nothing more. I'm all right with that, really. Some of those women you take home, though, have hopes of being more than a one-night stand. You're young, talented, famous, and extremely sexy. Who wouldn't want you? The point is, no one can have you—not completely. Not as long as Jessica Greenfield has this power over you. She has such a hold on your soul that she could never even begin to fathom its enormity. That isn't fair to those women you bring home, and it isn't fair to you either."

"So you advise me to grow up and move on?" Lynn's tone was flippant, though she really didn't mean it to be. Before Bri could respond, she continued. "Look, I had a crush on her in high school, but she is *not* the reason I'm not in a relationship. We've had this discussion before. I don't want to settle down, Bri. I like being single. I like the freedom that being single gives me."

"You keep telling yourself that." She shook her head and finally let go of Lynn's arm. "Maybe someday you'll convince yourself it's true."

"This is insane." Lynn stood and took her glass to the kitchen, wishing she'd never mentioned Jessie to Bri. Leave it to a therapist. Mention you're in love with someone once, and they'd never let it go. "Are you going to watch Oscar, or do I need to call someone else?"

"I'll do it, for you." Bri sighed as she looked at the cat, who was sitting in the window once again. "Go get dressed—and don't forget to bring your white T-shirt."

CHAPTER TWO

A t 4 Ladies, Saturday nights were always busy, but wet T-shirt contests brought out the lesbians from miles around. As a result, the bar was packed, wall-to-wall women of every kind, and all of them beautiful in their own way. Lynn and Bri shoved their way through the bodies to the bar, somehow managing to not get separated. They waited, successfully inching forward until they finally made it close enough to place their order.

"Hi, Renee!" Lynn said cheerily, moving in close enough that the bartender could hear her. "I'll have a shot and a beer, and a white wine for Bri."

Lynn rarely ordered anything other than wine, but when she did, Renee knew exactly what she wanted. As she got their drinks, Lynn watched her. Renee had been the first woman Lynn became involved with after moving to San Francisco almost fifteen years earlier. It had been a brief affair, but Renee had introduced Lynn to the local nightlife.

After setting the drinks on the bar in front of Lynn, Renee placed one hand over Lynn's as Lynn reached into her pocket with her other hand for some cash and shook her head. She tilted her chin toward the far end of the bar to her left, and Lynn looked in that direction. "You have an admirer."

"Wow, not *even* ten minutes." Bri bowed in reverence, and Lynn glanced at her, irritated. "Clearly I have underestimated your mighty powers of seduction. Please forgive me."

Lynn chose to ignore Bri for the moment. "Which one is it?"

"The really young one by herself down there," Renee said. "Green T-shirt, red hair in a ponytail. I've never seen her before, but she's paying for this round."

"Have you *ever* spent any money in this bar?" Bri joked.

"Not a dime."

"I can vouch for that." Renee tapped the back of Lynn's hand to get her attention again. "You should go introduce yourself, honey."

"I'll be right back." Lynn downed the shot of whiskey, then picked up her bottle of beer and pushed toward the end of the bar.

"I won't wait up!" Bri called before Lynn got too far away to hear the remark. Lynn simply waved over her shoulder without looking back.

It seemed to Lynn to take forever to reach the end of the bar. The mingled stench of cigarettes, beer, sweat, and perfume overwhelmed her. More than a few hands brushed her backside as she squeezed through the sea of women, not all of those touches accidental.

All kinds of women were there—some scantily clad, some wearing leather. A few wore makeup, but the majority didn't. A lot of them had on jeans and T-shirts, but some sported skirts or dresses. Several eyed Lynn appreciatively as she shoved past, but Lynn simply grinned and kept on moving. She loved the fact that women were attracted to her, and it really didn't matter to her if it was only because of the local fame she'd achieved as an author. A lot of these women knew who she was, and she played it for all it was worth.

"Thanks for the drink," Lynn said when she had finally reached the woman in the green T-shirt. She held out her hand in greeting. "I'm Lynn."

"Norah." A nervous smile pulled at Norah's lips when she briefly gripped Lynn's hand.

"I don't remember seeing you here before." Lynn casually rested an elbow on the bar and stood near her, to make conversation easier.

"It's my first time." Norah kept her attention on the bottle of beer sitting in front of her.

Lynn chuckled at the way the young woman avoided making

eye contact with anyone. The women in the bar *expected* to be looked at. After all, it was a pick-up joint.

"First time here," Lynn moved even closer, "or at *any* lesbian bar?"

"Is it that obvious?" Norah glanced away.

"Maybe a little. How old are you, anyway?"

Norah hesitated, and the tremulous smile wavered. Lynn considered walking away and forgetting about Norah, who was much too young. Deep down, Lynn's heart wasn't in it anyway. She couldn't seem to get Charlie's earlier news out of her mind. She found herself hoping against hope that Jessie and Wayne really had separated. Lynn shook her head and began to step back from the bar, but stopped when a hand gently gripped her forearm.

"Does it really matter?" Norah's tone and demeanor were much more confident. Lynn stepped back in, curious as to what Norah intended to say. She smiled seductively as she finally gave Lynn an appraising look. "I mean, we're two women who know what we want. Should age really be a factor?"

"Then tell me what *you* want, Norah." Lynn stood even closer so she could speak softly into Norah's ear. Norah was clearly hiding behind a brave façade, and Lynn quickly decided to call her on it. The timid young woman who only moments before had admitted to never being in a lesbian bar seemed far more real—and more appealing—to Lynn than the one full of false bravado.

She pulled back slightly and looked into Norah's eyes. That frightened girl was back, obviously not having expected Lynn to call her bluff. Lynn moved closer and, breathing softly into Norah's ear, spoke just loud enough to be heard over the pulsing dance music.

"What do you want, Norah?" Lynn grunted in satisfaction when Norah shuddered slightly. "Do you even know? Do you want to experiment, just to see what sex with another woman would be like? Do you want a one-night stand? Or are you looking for someone to share with your boyfriend? If it's the latter, I should tell you now, I'm not into men."

Hearing no response, Lynn backed away to get a better look

at Norah's face. Norah's confusion was clear in her expression and body language.

"How can you possibly know what you want when you can't even tell the one you supposedly want it from?" Lynn held up her beer bottle with a wry grin. "You're trying to pick *me* up, remember?"

"I'm sorry." Norah shook her head and stood to leave. It was Lynn's turn to stop her with a hand to her forearm.

"No, *I'm* sorry." Lynn could only hope she sounded as sincere as she felt. *Please tell me I'm not always this big of an ass.* Clearly she'd taken the game too far and didn't have enough sense to know when to back off.

"I'm twenty-one, all right?" Norah finally said. "I just wanted to see what this place was like, because I think I might be a lesbian. I *don't* have a boyfriend, and a one-night stand might be all I can handle."

Lynn seriously considered taking Norah home with her, but Charlie's phone call suddenly echoed in her head. She glanced out at the dance floor and tried to bring her thoughts back to the present. When she returned her attention to Norah, Lynn knew she'd be going home alone.

"Look, I really am sorry." Lynn urged her to take her seat again. "I'm having a bad day—hell, I'm having a bad *life*—and I shouldn't have taken it out on you. There are a lot of nice women out there. Unfortunately, at least for tonight, I'm not one of them. What made you pick me anyway? You could probably have your choice of just about anyone in this place. Frankly, I'm surprised you aren't already surrounded."

"I saw you walk in, and I was captivated," Norah said as she met Lynn's eyes. The music stopped suddenly—apparently it was time for the wet T-shirt contest to begin. "Haven't you ever seen someone and felt an instant attraction?"

"Yes," Lynn said, fighting an urge to glance over her shoulder at Bri. "Listen, if I were in a different state of mind, things would be different between us. But as I said, it's not a good night."

"Are you with the woman you came in with?" Norah indicated Bri, and Lynn finally did look in her direction, only to find that she was still in the same spot where she'd left her. "I think she's trying really hard not to stare at us."

"Bri likes to live vicariously through me." Lynn brought her attention back to Norah. "She's only a friend, but I really should be getting back over there."

"Can I give you my phone number?" Norah reached over the bar and grabbed a pen and a fresh napkin to write on. "In case you change your mind. I live alone."

Lynn waited patiently for her to write the number down, then watched Norah quickly leave the bar. Her mind wandered a bit, and her own words came back to haunt her—*How can you possibly know what you want when you can't even tell the one you supposedly want it from?*

"Is it possible that they've really separated?" she muttered under her breath, allowing the thought to truly take hold for the first time since Charlie's phone call. Maybe it wasn't simply a fantasy anymore. Maybe this was her chance to finally lay her cards on the table. She needed to know if there was a chance for anything between them. They'd shared a kiss once in high school after flirting with one another all year, and Lynn had never really given up hope that there could be more between them, that Jessie wasn't just flirting with the unknown.

"Get a grip," she said to herself. "Even if they have separated, there has to be a reason, and Jessie will be upset. I need to be a friend for her now, not another complication. And she's straight." Even as she spoke, her heart rebelled and she pressed her hand to it, as though she could keep it from splitting in half.

"Talking to yourself? That could seriously deplete your possible dating pool." Bri's voice came from directly behind her, rudely jerking her back from her musings. Lynn closed her eyes and took a deep breath before facing her. "She left awfully fast. Losing your touch, Romeo?"

"She came on strong, so I did too." Lynn forced a smile before swallowing the last of her beer and placing the empty bottle on the bar.

"So in other words, you scared her to death," Renee said as

she set another shot and a beer in front of Lynn with a wink. "From another admirer."

"Jesus," Bri muttered.

Lynn looked in the direction Renee indicated and saw an incredibly attractive brunette, much closer to Lynn's age than Norah had been, raising a glass her way and smiling. Lynn smiled back before picking up the shot glass and downing the whiskey, then half of the beer. She lifted the bottle in a gesture of gratitude toward the woman who'd paid for it, then set it down in front of Renee.

"I'm going home."

"Alone?" Bri and Renee said in unison.

"I'm not in the mood." She just wanted to get to Portland and see Jessie. She had to know what was going on. She couldn't, *wouldn't*, examine it too closely, but she had to be there in case Jessie needed someone to talk to. Needed *her*. "If I had been, I probably would have taken advantage of that sweet young thing."

Just before Lynn walked away, she heard Bri say to Renee, "Since when is she not in the mood?"

Lynn chose to ignore the comment, because it was true. She was *always* in the mood. Charlie's phone call had put her life in a tailspin, whether she wanted to admit it or not. She did her best not to think about the reasons she was going home alone.

Chapter Three

Jessica Greenfield glanced at her watch again, wondering where in the world her sister was. She sat back in her chair and took a good look around the bar Sarah had named The Living Room. It was a Tuesday night, and the place was deserted. Two women were playing pool in the corner, and one guy was watching the basketball game from a seat at the bar.

Her sister, Karen, had invited her out for a drink, and now it appeared as if she was being stood up. With a sigh, she looked over her shoulder and saw Sarah, Karen's partner of the last ten years, heading her way.

"Jess, Karen just called, and she's hung up with a client." Sarah looked apologetic, and Jessie simply nodded. Unfortunately, she was used to it. "She's—"

"Really sorry, I know. Such is the life of a corporate attorney." Jessie picked up her purse and started to stand, but she stopped when Sarah took a seat across from her. "Aren't you working?"

"We're dead tonight." Sarah looked around at the three people in the bar before returning her attention to Jessie with a shrug. "I'm thinking about reducing the hours and only opening Thursday through Sunday. So, if you don't mind the company, I'm yours—at least until somebody needs a refill."

Jessie didn't know what to say. Karen had invited her here to talk about Wayne. Sarah and Karen had told her they'd had misgivings about him before they got married, but she'd refused to listen. She concentrated on the scotch on the rocks in front of her.

"Has he been bothering you again?" Sarah asked, placing a hand on top of Jessie's. "You know you can come and stay with us, right? We love you and Amber, and in spite of what you think, you wouldn't be in the way."

"He's in Las Vegas." Jessie shook her head and fought the tears that threatened to fall. She hated becoming so sensitive during the past few months. She cried about almost anything lately. She hated Wayne for pushing all her buttons and forcing her to live her life as an emotional bundle of nerves, and for making her feel weak. "I refuse to let him have enough power to push me around anymore, but the house is in his name. When he finishes this job in Vegas and is back in town, I may want Amber to stay with you for a while. A six-year-old little girl shouldn't have to deal with all this crap."

"Whatever you need, honey, you know that." Sarah removed her hand and sat back in her seat while she watched Jessie with obvious concern. Jessie squirmed under the scrutiny. "Has he been in contact with you?"

"He tries, but I don't answer the cell when he calls." Jessie met Sarah's eyes. The sympathy she saw there made her look away again with a short laugh. Jesus, how had her mother dealt with it for so many years? "I really need to get caller ID on the landline, though. I could kick myself whenever I answer it and it's him."

"Does he know about the restraining order?"

"I told him, but he doesn't care. Apparently his lawyer hasn't informed him of it yet." Jessie took a big slug of the scotch and closed her eyes as it burned its way down her throat. When she opened them again, she tucked an annoying strand of hair behind her ears and met Sarah's gaze. "But he's really going to freak when he finds out about the divorce."

"When do you see the lawyer about that?"

"Tomorrow morning." Jessie nodded when Sarah held up a finger to let her know she needed to get something for a customer. While she was gone, Jessie let out a big breath, absently running her finger along the rim of her glass. Why hadn't she listened when Karen, Sarah, and even Lynn had voiced their doubts about her marrying Wayne? For God's sake, her parents had been the only ones who *did* approve of him. That should have been a ripped-up red flag.

But things hadn't always been bad between them. He'd been the perfect boyfriend, and when they married almost eight years ago, he'd been the perfect husband—at least for a while. He'd been attentive, and loving, and wanted to spend every possible moment with her. Not long after they were married, though, he'd pushed for her to give up her career as a freelance graphic artist. Luckily she'd kept in touch with many of her former clients, and now that she was on her own again, a few of them were beginning to give her more and more work.

But when she got pregnant things had really begun to change. Wayne started spending more time away from home, and though Jessie suspected he was having an affair, she never confronted him. Truthfully, part of her *wanted* him to be having an affair. Their relationship had been slowly falling apart, and it would have made a break between them so much easier. She'd never felt what people described as love—that weak-kneed, head-over-heels feeling with him—and after she got pregnant, she was happy when he didn't come home, preferring her own company to his overbearing presence.

When Amber was born, Wayne seemed to revert back to his old self, and they were once again a fairly happy couple. He spent more time at home and always helped with the baby. They renewed their friendship, although what little passion that had existed between them had vanished. When Amber turned two, he changed again, almost overnight. He started hanging out with some of the guys from work, and if Jessie had known at the time that he'd started doing drugs, she'd have kicked him out. As it turned out, she hadn't found out about the drugs until a few months before she ended up in the hospital.

Jessie hated to admit to herself that she was scared about the future. If Wayne could dupe her so easily into thinking he was a wonderful, caring man, what chance did she have with anyone else? Was she doomed to repeat the same mistakes her mother had made? She sat up a little straighter as she reminded herself she'd kicked Wayne out. That alone made her infinitely stronger than her mother had ever been. Jessie would *never* allow anyone to hurt her daughter.

"Sorry about that." Sarah again took a seat and set a new glass of scotch in front of Jessie.

Jessie waved away the apology. "No problem." Just then her cell phone on the table began to vibrate and she jumped, her pulse quickening. She slowly reached for it, praying it wouldn't be Wayne. When she turned it over and saw *Lynn Patrick* on the display, she relaxed and let out her breath. She shook her head at Sarah's worried expression. "It's Lynn."

"I'll be right back." Sarah stood and went back to the bar to give her some privacy.

"Hey, Jess." Lynn's sultry, low voice hummed in her ear, and Jessie closed her eyes, letting the sound warm her much like the alcohol had done. "How's my favorite person in the whole world?"

"Better now," Jessie replied with a smile. It surprised her that she did indeed feel calmer just from hearing the sound of Lynn's voice. "Are you in town?"

"Yep, and I'm all settled in at Casa Patrick." Lynn laughed. "God, you have no idea what it's like spending three weeks with my parents. I love them, but they do get on my nerves. And then there's Mom, always trying to orchestrate my love life. She's hoping I'll find a nice woman in town and settle down."

"Would that really be so bad?" Jessie asked, thinking it would be nice to have Lynn around all the time. She had begun looking forward to December more each year, because she loved the time they spent together. "Moving back here, I mean."

"No, not if I found the right woman, I guess." Lynn's voice sounded almost wistful, and Jessie wondered why. She chuckled softly when she heard Lynn's mother's muffled voice in the background. Lynn apparently took the phone from her ear and put a hand over the mouthpiece. "Just a minute, Mom." Jessie waited patiently, amused at the way some things never changed. "Christ, I can't even get a minute of peace in the bathroom."

"You can come stay with me if you want." Jessie made the offer before her brain had the opportunity to engage, but the stillness from the other end gave her time to think about her proposal. It wasn't a bad idea, really. She had an extra bedroom and would feel infinitely better having another adult in the house.

"What about Wayne?" Lynn finally asked.

"He's working in Las Vegas for a few weeks." Charlie had undoubtedly already given his sister that bit of information, judging by the twinkle in his eye when she'd told him the other day in the grocery store. "He's not supposed to be back until the second or third week in January."

"It's very tempting, but I'm not sure my mother would be happy about it. And, trust me, when Mama Patrick isn't happy, nobody's happy. Besides, for some reason she likes having me around. Can we talk about it over dinner tomorrow night?"

"My place at six?"

"I'll be there."

Jessie pushed the End Call button and wondered why her stomach was fluttering. She reacted that way a lot when she had plans with Lynn. She shook her head and started to put the phone in her purse, but frowned when she brushed the cold steel of the .38 caliber gun she kept in there. She jerked away and studied her hands, which had totally lost their golden summer tan. She tried to compose herself when Sarah took a seat across from her once again.

"When are you going to see her?" Sarah asked.

"She's coming for dinner tomorrow." Jessie took a swallow of her drink and tried to make her hands stop shaking.

"Did you tell her what happened?"

"No, and I'm not planning to." Jessie stared at Sarah defiantly. "Promise me you won't say anything either."

"Hon, she'll see the scar on your cheek and notice that you favor your left arm. Why not let her know what happened?"

"Did Karen ever tell you about the time when Lynn stood up to our father?" Jessie waited until Sarah shook her head, then continued. "We were juniors in high school, and Karen had just come out to them. He caught Lynn and me in the backyard hugging. She was holding me because I was so upset about my father kicking

Karen out and my mother doing nothing to stop it. He came out there yelling at the top of his lungs about what perverts we were. Lynn let go of me, then stepped between my father and me. He called Lynn a fucking dyke, and when she didn't deny it, he got even more pissed off. He reached for me, but she grabbed his wrist and twisted his arm until he fell to his knees."

"Oh, shit," Sarah murmured with a grimace, obviously knowing what was coming next.

"Yeah." Jessie laughed humorlessly. "As soon as she let go, he got up and punched her in the face. God, she had a black eye for weeks. Anyway, he obviously thought he'd won, but she was on him again so quick, he didn't know how to react. He wasn't used to a woman fighting back—especially a sixteen-year-old girl. I was scared out of my mind, because she had him by the shirt collar and they fell backward, Lynn sitting on his chest. She told him that if he ever laid a finger on me again, she'd kill him herself. Her parents pressed charges against him when they found out what happened, and things actually did get better for me after that. He decided to take out all of his frustrations on my mother instead."

"And that's why you won't tell her about Wayne putting you in the hospital for over a week?" Sarah didn't seem to understand where Jessie was coming from. Jessie sighed and took another drink. "I'm sorry, honey, I know that was an awful thing that happened, but I still think you should let her know."

"Why, Sarah? So she can go after Wayne and threaten to kill him too? Or, worse, actually do it? Hasn't there been enough violence in my life?" Jessie had to work at keeping her voice down because of the lack of background noise to drown out their conversation. She leaned toward Sarah and spoke more quietly. "Jesus, I *know* Wayne. He wouldn't be content with only a black eye."

"Jess, give her a little more credit than that. Even though a brash sixteen-year-old did something that reckless, a thirty-three-year-old woman wouldn't necessarily do something equally stupid. And if you had someone else on your side through this, we'd all feel a lot better about where things are going with him."

"I couldn't live with myself if something happened to her."

There. She'd said it out loud. "She hates him, Sarah. And he certainly isn't fond of her either. He hated it when she came home for three weeks every year."

"Yet *you* look forward to it," Sarah said gently. Jessie met her eyes and waited for more, but nothing followed.

"I miss her. I'd feel a lot better if my best friend lived close by."

"Are you sure that's all she is to you?"

"What are you getting at?" They stared at each other—Jessie waiting for some kind of explanation and Sarah obviously waiting for her meaning to dawn on Jessie. It struck her then what Sarah was saying, and her cheeks warmed. "Are you insinuating that I might feel more for her than friendship?"

"I'm not insinuating anything." Sarah's smug smile hinted otherwise, and Jessie wasn't sure if she should be angry or embarrassed. "I'm only saying you should think about it. I can see where you might be confused, having an overbearing father and given the experience Karen went through when she came out. If you *had* ever experienced any feelings like that, it would have been natural to suppress them."

"Jesus Christ." Jessie folded her arms on the table and rested her forehead on them, shaking her head slowly. "I've finally stopped my mother from trying to persuade me to work harder at pleasing Wayne, and now you're trying to drag me out of a closet I'm not in."

"Are you sure about that?" Sarah was grinning when Jessie raised her head again. "I've seen the way some of these women look at you in here, and I've even watched you look back at a few. You can't tell me it's never crossed your mind."

It had crossed Jessie's mind, on more than one occasion, but she'd never shared it with anyone. Should she confide in Sarah? Well, what did she have to lose? She took a deep breath.

"If I tell you something I've never told another living soul, will you promise it'll go no further than this table?" Jessie waited, and Sarah nodded. "Not even Karen can know."

"Ooh, this is juicy. I can't wait." Sarah rubbed her hands

together. When Jessie grabbed her forearm and stared at her, Sarah finally nodded again. She even crossed her heart. "I promise."

"During our senior year in high school, when Lynn told me she was a lesbian, I kissed her." Jessie waited for the ribbing to start, but she saw nothing other than surprise in Sarah's eyes. "Say something."

"I'm…" Sarah stammered as she shrugged and shook her head. Jessie had finally silenced the ever-witty Sarah, who always seemed to have a comeback for everything thrown her way. "Wow. I definitely did not see that coming. How was it?"

"Horrible." Jessie laughed and released her hold on Sarah's arm. "It was awkward, and sloppy, and neither one of us ever mentioned it again."

"Was it your first kiss?"

"Yes."

"Hers too?"

"I don't know. I never asked."

"Wow," Sarah said again. "Your first kiss was with a girl. See, you just might be in that closet. I'm sure since then you've both gotten better at kissing—at least I'd hope so. Maybe you should give it another shot before you completely rule it out."

"I am *not* in the closet." Jessie said in a dismissive tone—and volume—as she yanked on her jacket and headed for the door.

"But if you find out that you are, I want to be the first to know," Sarah called to her.

Jessie stepped aside when a woman came through the doors to the bar. Before she could stop herself, she watched her saunter past, drawn in by the way her hips moved. She glanced back at a smirking Sarah, shook her head, and flipped Sarah the bird before leaving the bar.

CHAPTER FOUR

Jessie already had dinner made when Lynn rang the doorbell at five minutes after six the next evening. She chuckled because Lynn never made it anywhere on time. Often, she'd jokingly told Lynn she'd be late to her own funeral. Jessie took the last sip of her glass of wine and went to open the door, ignoring the swarm of butterflies attacking her stomach.

Lynn was grinning widely, and Jessie's breath caught. It wasn't possible, but Lynn looked even more attractive than Jessie remembered. If Jessie *was* a lesbian, as Sarah had not so subtly suggested, she wouldn't hesitate to get involved with Lynn. But she wasn't, of course.

"You're certainly a sight for sore eyes," Lynn said. She hugged Jessie tight.

"You too." Jessie held on a little longer than necessary. She took a deep breath of musky cologne mingled with herbal shampoo—the scents she always associated with Lynn. After she finally pulled away she took the brown bag she assumed contained a bottle of whiskey, their drink of choice whenever they got together. "You can put your coat in the closet."

"Where's my favorite little girl?" Lynn asked when she joined Jessie in the kitchen.

"My mother took Amber on a trip to see Mickey Mouse." Jessie grabbed a couple of plates from the cupboard and set them on the counter. She winced slightly at the lingering pain in her left shoulder, but managed to hide it from Lynn since her back was to her.

"California or Florida?"

"Florida. They left last night, and they'll be gone two weeks."

"Nice. I'd love to go to Florida."

"Mom wanted me to go with them." Jessie avoided looking directly at Lynn, because she didn't want her to see the small, one-inch scar on her cheek. She cursed herself for not waiting until after the holidays to get her hair cut, because now it was just long enough to reach her shoulders. She'd tried to style it so it'd cover the scar below her eye, but nothing she did looked natural. It had reminded her of a balding man with a comb-over. Anyway, she was being ridiculous, because she couldn't possibly avoid looking at Lynn the entire evening.

"Why didn't you?" Lynn opened the cupboard and got out two shot glasses.

"I wanted to see you." Her simple explanation was the truth. Jessie hadn't really thought about it at the time, but that was indeed the reason she'd declined her mother's invitation to join them, although she'd told her mother she needed some time alone to recharge her batteries. She wasn't sure if she should confide in her mother about the impending divorce yet. Considering that she'd stayed with Jessie's father for years, she might expect Jessie to do the same. Jessie did her best not to cringe at the possibility.

"That's nice." Lynn's voice was soft, and Jessie took the offered shot glass, downing the contents quickly. "Another?"

"Not now." Jessie turned to look at her, and the amused smile on Lynn's face faded as her eyes settled on the spot just below Jessie's left eye. Jessie glanced away, but Lynn put down the bottle and, with two fingers under Jessie's chin, forced her head back to get a better look.

"What happened to you?" Lynn's voice was a mixture of concern and the restrained anger Jessie had come to know so well when they talked about Jessie's parents. Jessie closed her eyes when Lynn gently rubbed her thumb along the scar.

"It's nothing." Jessie's voice caught as she recalled how the scar came to be, but she pulled away from Lynn and turned her attention back to dinner. She wasn't surprised when her attempt to dissuade Lynn from further questioning didn't work.

"Jessie, please talk to me." Lynn placed a gentle hand on Jessie's forearm and squeezed. "What happened?"

"I walked into a door." Jessie forced a smile, but Lynn's expression never changed. Jessie's eyes watered and she shook her head. "You were right about Wayne."

"He hit you?" Lynn's voice was soft, but her blue eyes conveyed anger. Jessie put a hand over Lynn's, which was still on her arm. "When did this happen?"

Jessie closed her eyes, trying to dispel the images of that horrible night. When she opened them again, Lynn was still studying her face.

"About eight months ago."

During their awkward silence, Jessie forced herself not to look away from Lynn's darkening stare.

"Please tell me he spent time in jail for this." Lynn's voice had a hard edge, causing a chill to spread through Jessie's body. "Because if he didn't, I'll kill him."

"He got permission from his parole officer to take the job in Vegas." Jessie pulled her arm away and took a step back. She really didn't want to discuss Wayne this evening. She also hoped that by omitting the truth—by letting Lynn think he was on parole—Lynn would assume he'd done jail time. Actually, because it was his first offense, he'd only received probation. He had to report to the courts every couple of weeks for the next year, but other than that, he was free. That was why Jessie had finally purchased a gun, something only her attorney and Karen knew about. If Wayne intended to come back and cause problems, she'd damn well be prepared to deal with him. "I have a restraining order that keeps him away, and I filed for divorce this morning. I expect he won't be too happy about that. You know, I really don't want to discuss it, okay? Can we just have a nice quiet dinner and talk about you tonight?"

A myriad of emotions stormed through Lynn's eyes, but she finally rested her hip against the counter and forced a smile. Jessie let out a sigh and turned back to preparing dinner.

"That's fine, but I want to hear about it sometime, so you're only getting a temporary reprieve." Lynn twisted the cap off a bottle of beer and took a long drink. Jessie wasn't surprised at the declaration, but she was dreading having to admit to Lynn the severity of what Wayne had done. "And I'll also want to hear your reasons for not telling me about this sooner."

❖

During dinner—Jessie's famous pot roast with mashed potatoes and string beans—Lynn forced herself to talk about what was going on in her life. Deadlines weren't an exciting topic, so they turned their attention to Charlie's marital woes. But Lynn's anger seethed just under the surface. How the hell could anyone hit Jessie? And why hadn't anyone bothered to tell her about it when it happened?

"Have you thought about my offer?" Jessie asked while they washed the dishes after they'd eaten. "About staying here with me for part of the month?"

"Yeah, about that…" Lynn played with the dishtowel she held, folding and unfolding it. "I'm not sure that would be such a good idea."

"Why not?" Jessie laughed, but couldn't disguise the hurt in her voice. "I'm here all alone, and I *do* have an extra bedroom. Your mother drives you crazy, so why not stay here, at least for a few days?"

Lynn looked up and, for the first time, noticed a Rose's Bakery box on the counter. She did a mental cheer for the diversion.

"Oh, wow," she said, picking it up. "Please tell me this is my favorite seven-layer chocolate cake."

"It is. I bought it just for you this afternoon when I was out."

They got plates, dished out two slices, then retreated to the living room, each with a beer in hand. When Lynn took the first bite, she closed her eyes and let the rich chocolate take over her senses.

"Sweet Jesus, that's delicious. If you weren't straight, I'd ask you to marry me." Lynn held her breath for a moment after the words escaped and chastised herself for letting the Freudian thought slip out. Neither of them said anything as they finished their dessert.

Lynn sat back and watched Jessie, wondering why she had blushed at the words. When Jessie finally sat back as well, Lynn filled their shot glasses and handed one to Jessie.

"True confessions," Jessie said, without looking at her.

"What?"

"True confessions," Jessie repeated. "We used to play it when we were kids. Please don't tell me you don't remember?"

"Of course I remember." Lynn had always hated the game. It was like truth or dare, only without the opportunity to take a dare—you only had to answer the question honestly. It was a stupid juvenile game, and—

"I'll even let you ask the first question."

Lynn looked up in mid-thought. This could be the perfect opportunity to broach the subject she needed to talk about yet had nervously avoided all evening. Not being able to find the right moment to initiate it without the game irritated her. She *never* had a problem letting a woman know when she was interested. When Jessie looked at her, waiting for her to ask a question, her heart rate accelerated to a dangerously high level.

"Fine." Lynn sat up straight, a hand on each knee, and took a deep breath to calm herself. It would be harder than she thought. Jessie's light brown eyes bored into her, waiting for the question Lynn was having trouble putting into words. "Okay, here goes. Have you ever…have you…shit, I can't do this."

Sweat was forming on her upper lip, and she turned to face the bookshelf across the room. When Jessie touched her knee, she jumped, but forced a laugh to cover her nervousness. She couldn't do it. Jessie didn't need the stress of having Lynn wanting more from her. Wayne had managed to turn her life upside down, and Jessie didn't need any more complications.

"Lynn, you can ask me anything you want. We're friends. Nothing you ask will shock me."

"Do you miss Wayne?" Lynn asked the question while thinking something very different, keeping her eyes on the bookcase across the room.

When no answer came, Lynn looked at her. Jessie appeared surprised and perhaps disappointed. The quiet stretched between them, and Lynn fought to not squirm under Jessie's inspection.

"No." Jessie's voice was quiet, and as soon as she spoke, she looked away and downed a shot of whiskey. "I'm surprised you'd even ask. He's been out of my life for eight months now, and I'm through with him, Lynn."

"I'm sorry." Lynn shook her head and watched Jessie until she finally turned her head back toward Lynn. "But you have to admit it's a valid question, Jess. Your mother never left your father when he hit her."

"I'm not my mother." Jessie sounded perturbed, but apparently didn't intend to let Lynn's insensitivity ruin the game for her. "My turn now?"

"Now I remember why I hate this fucking game. It does nothing but cause animosity between the participants." Lynn flopped back and closed her eyes. Jessie laughed, but Lynn refused to look at her. "Ask your damn question."

"Do you have a girlfriend?"

Her eyes popped open and she stared at Jessie. Jessie had never asked her that before. She was almost certain she'd heard the question wrong, but the look in Jessie's eyes told her she hadn't. This was the best opportunity she'd ever get to tell Jessie how she felt, and she was going to pass on it.

"No, I don't." Lynn was surprised she could hear herself answer the question since her pulse was pounding so loudly in her ears.

"That's too bad, Lynn." Jessie hesitated, obviously searching for the right words. Lynn didn't even think when she placed a hand on Jessie's knee, encouraging her to continue. "You deserve to have happiness in your life."

"So do you, Jess, and you'll have it someday. It may not seem like it now, but you're too wonderful to be alone for long."

Jessie felt something stir deep inside while they sat there staring at each other—that truly exhilarating feeling of discovering one's most hidden desires. She needed to look away from Lynn, yet at the same time, she couldn't. The raw need to connect physically with another person was totally foreign.

"Gee, that was a fun game." Lynn was the one to finally break the silence with her sarcastic remark. She glanced at her watch, obviously not expecting Jessie to respond. "Oh, my God, look at the time. I should probably get home."

She stood, but Jessie grabbed her wrist and pulled her back down. Lynn landed with one arm over the back of the couch, Jessie still grasping her wrist. Their thighs touched, but neither of them attempted to move apart.

"Okay, maybe it's not so late." Lynn's tremulous smile gave away her nervousness.

Jessie briefly wondered if the alcohol they'd consumed was giving her the courage to do what she wanted, *needed*, to do. Lynn didn't pull away when Jessie gently pushed the hair from her face.

Jessie wasn't entirely sure which of them moved first. She only knew for certain that her lips brushed Lynn's. It scared her, but at the same time, she'd never been so excited. They both backed away tentatively, then Lynn's hand was on Jessie's cheek. Jessie relaxed into the touch as she watched Lynn's eyes drop to her lips.

"This is crazy, Jess." Her voice was rough with what Jessie hoped was desire, and then Lynn returned her eyes to Jessie's. "We shouldn't be doing this."

"Why?" Jessie was trembling slightly, and she didn't try to hide her nervousness. She couldn't, even if she'd wanted to. "It feels good, doesn't it?"

"Yes, it does. And that's precisely why. If it feels this good, it could lead to other things."

"Would that be so bad?" Jessie waited for a response, but Lynn continued to stare at her with an unnerving calmness. The depth of emotion in Lynn's expression terrified Jessie, but the alcohol had lowered her inhibitions.

The second time, Jessie knew which of them initiated the kiss. She placed a hand on Lynn's thigh and slowly leaned into her. Lynn half-heartedly resisted, but Jessie allowed her to take control. The feel of Lynn's tongue sliding along her own sent tendrils of fire straight to her groin, and she moaned into Lynn's mouth. Jessie let her hand touch Lynn's breast and linger there, not quite sure what to do now that she had reached her destination.

Lynn was the one who finally stopped the kiss by gently pushing Jessie's shoulders. They continued looking into one another's eyes, both of them out of breath. Lynn gently took Jessie's hand from her breast and held it.

"What's wrong?" Jessie could sense Lynn's confusion and wanted to say so many things, but she couldn't form the words.

"It's late," Lynn said, resting her forehead against Jessie's. "Maybe we both need to sleep this off, Jess."

"I'm sorry," Jessie said, feeling as if she might cry. "I didn't mean to—"

"God, no, Jessie, I'm the one who's sorry." Lynn backed away slightly and moved her hand to Jessie's cheek, pushing the hair away from Jessie's eyes as she spoke. "This shouldn't have happened. Not like this, anyway."

"I don't want you to leave," Jessie said when Lynn stood once again. This neediness was new to her and she wasn't entirely sure she liked it. "Spend the night with me."

"I can't." Lynn touched her lips briefly to the top of Jessie's head before walking away.

"Why did you say it wouldn't be a good idea for you to stay here with me while you're in town?" Jessie asked. She fought back the tears that threatened. The one person she'd thought she could always count on had rejected her. Lynn returned and crouched in front of her, holding one of Jessie's hands between both of hers.

"Listen to me, Jess," Lynn didn't speak until Jessie met her eyes, "I can't stay here because of what just happened. I'm a lesbian, and you're not. Wayne hates me, and if he found out I was here, you'd have more trouble with him than you're already dealing with. You're going through a rough time right now, and I want to be your friend. I'll be here if you need me, but I can't stay in the same house with you."

"But I want you to."

"We've been drinking. If you still feel this way in the morning, we can talk about it again, all right?"

"Come by for lunch tomorrow. One o'clock?" Jessie really didn't want the night to end. She was afraid if she let Lynn walk out the door, she might never see her again.

"I'll bring Chinese," Lynn said. Jessie raised their hands and kissed the back of Lynn's. "Get some sleep."

After Lynn disappeared out the front door, Jessie picked up her half bottle of beer. Exactly what had just happened?

She'd thrown herself at Lynn like some sex-starved slut, that's what had happened. She raised two fingers to lips still tingling from their kiss and sighed. Sarah was right. It was much better this time around.

Chapter Five

Lynn drove home in a haze, trying not to think about that kiss, because if she did, she'd end up driving off the road. When she turned onto her parents' street, she shook her head. *Jessica Greenfield kissed me. Again. Definitely better this time.*

The kitchen light was on, and she glanced at the clock on the car's CD player. It was after ten, which meant her father was already in bed and her mother was sitting in the kitchen waiting for her. She checked her reflection in the rearview mirror, feeling as though she was seventeen again and her mother would be able to see that she'd been making out.

She went straight to the kitchen, where her mother had a fresh pot of coffee sitting by the sink and a magazine spread before her.

"Care to join me?" Rose Patrick asked without looking up. She didn't wait for an answer, but stood and walked to the pot to pour another cup.

"Sure, why not?" Lynn took a seat as her mother placed the coffee in front of her. When Rose sat once again, Lynn took her hand. "Is something wrong? I know ten o'clock isn't late by most people's standards, but you've been going to bed the same time as Dad for as long as I can remember. I hope you weren't waiting up for me."

"Nothing's wrong. I couldn't sleep." Rose passed her the cream and sugar, then took a sip from her own cup.

"You're sure nothing's wrong?" Lynn had always been proud of her relationship with her mother. In high school, when all her friends were bitching about how horrible their parents were, Lynn could never find anything bad to say about hers. She'd always been able to talk about anything with her mother.

"I'm worried about you, Lynn."

Lynn studied her mother's face. Although she was close to sixty, she could easily pass for forty-five. Nobody ever believed they were mother and daughter.

"About me? Why?"

"You're thirty-three, honey, and you're still alone." Rose shrugged as she directed her blue eyes to Lynn's face. They were the same intense color as Lynn's own, and her mother still had the coal-black hair that Lynn had inherited as well. She hoped she wouldn't have a single gray hair at sixty either. "I don't like to think about you all alone down there in California. When are you going to find a nice young woman to settle down with? I wouldn't be opposed to you making me a grandmother again, either. I love Charlie's kids, but I want more."

Lynn smiled, warmed inside. Rose asked about any possible new partners every time they saw each other. The grandmother thing, though—that was new. The sincerity in her mother's tone touched Lynn.

"I'm fine, Mom. Someday I'll find a woman with enough tolerance to put up with all my shit, and you'll be the first to know. But as far as the grandchildren are concerned—maybe you should go back and read those biology textbooks you teach from. You're going to have some rather confused students."

"You know what I mean." Rose laughed, her eyes full of affection. "I wasn't born yesterday. I know all about artificial insemination, and adoption's always a possibility, you know."

"Or I could find some woman who already has a kid," Lynn suggested, and couldn't help but laugh at her mother's obvious anticipation.

"Oh? Do you have someone in mind?"

"No," Lynn said sadly, recalling the kiss earlier that evening. She tried not to squirm as her mother watched her intently. "What?"

"How's Jessie doing?"

Lynn flinched. Could her mother read her mind?

"Do you know what Wayne did to her?" Lynn asked, trying to steer the topic away from *her* and Jessie.

"She told you?" Rose seemed surprised, and when Lynn nodded, her mother seemed to relax. "Thank God, because I wasn't sure how much longer I could keep from filling you in myself."

"Wait—you *did* know, and you didn't tell me?" Lynn tensed. Rose obviously regretted her admission.

"Karen called me when Jessie was taken to the hospital. She wanted me to bring their mother."

Lynn's stomach dropped. She could see her mother's mouth moving, but her pulse was pounding so loud in her head that she couldn't hear anything. Jessie had been in the hospital, and no one had bothered to inform her? She closed her eyes and tried to calm her racing heart as the room began to spin. After a moment, she felt her mother's hand on her arm.

"Lynn, sweetie, what is it? Are you all right?"

"The hospital?" Her voice sounded far away, even to her own ears.

"You said she told you."

"She said Wayne hit her, and then she wouldn't discuss it anymore." Lynn stared at her mother, trying hard not to let her anger show. "How could you keep this from me?"

"She asked me to. She said she wanted to tell you herself, in her own time. I figured since she was going to be okay it wasn't a big deal."

"Not a big deal? Are you serious? What if she'd died, Mom? Would you have told me about it then?" She shouldn't be angry at her mother, but she couldn't stop herself.

"Look how you're reacting now, eight months after the fact," Rose pointed out, showing a bit of uncharacteristic anger herself. "Jessie never forgave herself for what happened between you and her father. She was worried about you going off half-cocked and doing something stupid. Frankly, I was too, because I can see how much you care about her, Lynn. I'd have to be stupid to not know you're in love with her. And I know you know it, although why you've never told your family is beyond me. If I'd let you know, you'd have caught the next plane up here and probably killed that asshole. Not that he doesn't deserve it, but he's not worth the time you'd spend in prison."

Lynn didn't know what to say, because her mother was right. Her temper wasn't something she was proud of, but she'd always been protective of Jessie. *Admit it, you're* overprotective *of her.* Always had been and probably always would be. At the moment, though, she was more embarrassed than angry.

"How could you possibly know I'm in love with her?"

"I'm your mother, Lynn," Rose said, as if that simple statement explained everything. "Maybe someday you'll have a daughter and you'll understand. Until then, trust me. A mother knows everything. Have you ever told Jessie how you feel?"

"No, I haven't." Lynn sighed. "But she kissed me tonight. And she asked me to spend the night with her."

"Then why in God's name are you here talking to me?"

Lynn laughed. Leave it to her mother to cut to the chase.

"I didn't want alcohol to play any role in it." Lynn met her mother's bemused look and hoped she understood. "I've never been in love with anyone else, Mom. I don't know how it's all supposed to work, but if she and I ever get together, I want both of us to have full control of our faculties. Not to mention the shit she's going through with her asshole husband. She needs a friend right now, Mom. I can't throw this on her plate too. And I never told you guys because I didn't have anything to tell. No matter how much I wanted anything to happen, nothing ever did. It wasn't that I didn't trust my family to deal with it."

"My little girl's growing up." Rose smiled and took a sheet of paper from the counter. "Here's that list of things I wanted you to get at the grocery store tomorrow. You do remember that I asked you to go, don't you?"

"Yes, Mother." Truthfully, she hadn't remembered, because she hadn't been able to think about anything all evening but Jessie. Rose kissed her on the cheek, then squeezed her shoulder.

"You stink of alcohol." She wrinkled her nose at the odor and smiled. "Get some sleep, and I'll see you in the morning."

Lynn stared at her mother's back until Rose disappeared up the stairs. She poured herself another cup of coffee before shutting off the pot and returning to her seat at the table. As she stirred in the cream and sugar she watched the liquid swirl.

The kiss was still haunting her. It had been unbelievably exciting, and she felt so guilty for letting it happen. She could still taste Jessie now as she slowly ran her tongue along her lips. Did Jessie have any idea how she affected her? The look in Jessie's eyes just before they kissed indicated that she did know, but what if it *had* been the alcohol speaking for Jessie? Or maybe Jessie simply needed the alcohol to give her the courage she needed to kiss Lynn. With other women, those things had never mattered. With Jessie, though, it was *all* that mattered.

She groaned quietly and laid her head down on the table, clasping her hands in her lap.

"You are so pathetic, Patrick," she said. It was odd enough that a single kiss had excited her so much, because that hadn't happened in years. But even stranger, while she was sitting here in her mother's kitchen, her body was reacting much the same way it had when Jessie parted her lips to allow Lynn's tongue in.

She sat up suddenly and crossed her legs, squeezing them tight and closing her eyes against the onslaught of feeling. "Damn it."

CHAPTER SIX

Jessie woke the next morning even more confused than she'd been the night before. After showering and dressing, she went downstairs and sat on the couch. In the bookshelf across the room were four books that she hadn't owned before her hospital stay, two of them by author Lynn Patrick.

She raised her fingers to her mouth, still feeling the press of Lynn's lips on her own. She closed her eyes and thought about the ramifications of that kiss. Certainly it was more significant than the one they'd shared so many years before. Back then, they had been young and impetuous. Now they were adults and their actions had consequences. She was married, for God's sake, and had a child. True, the marriage was over, but until a few months before, she'd assumed she was straight.

Jessie retrieved one of Lynn's books from the shelf and flipped through it. She'd read it while she was in the hospital and wondered if Lynn was writing about her. Jessie had *hoped* she was. That realization should have scared her, but it didn't. Surprisingly, the first sex scene had aroused her so much that she began flirting with the possibility she might be attracted to women. But she'd never acted on it until last night.

The phone rang and she dropped the book.

"Hello." She tried to calm her racing heart.

"Good morning, sunshine." Jessie cringed at the sound of Wayne's voice. "How are you this beautiful morning?"

"Wayne, you need to stop calling here. I can have phone calls added to the restraining order if I need to." Jessie amazed herself at how unruffled she sounded, because she certainly didn't feel that way.

"Baby, I need to talk to you and I don't want to do this through lawyers," he said. "I told you I was sorry about what happened. Let me come back home to you when this job's over."

"You were sorry the first time it happened too, Wayne, but that didn't stop you from doing it again, did it? I refuse to subject my daughter to the same things I grew up with. I told you that when we first got married." She should hang up on him, but part of her feared retaliation if she pissed him off. "If you really want the house back, I'll move out so you can live here, but you will *not* be coming home to Amber and me."

"Jessie, you don't know what you're saying, baby. I've changed. I've gone to counseling."

"Only because the court ordered you to." She fought to keep her voice down so he wouldn't know how much he was getting to her.

"But I did do it. We can work this out if you'll only give me a chance."

"I'm hanging up now, Wayne. Don't call here again."

"Jess..." was the last thing she heard before pushing the Off button and slamming the receiver down on the coffee table. She had her head in her hands when the phone rang again.

"What part of *do not call here again* did you not understand?" she yelled as she brought the phone to her ear again. The lack of noise on the other end unnerved her. Was he outside the house, taunting her? She was about to go check the front door when she heard a quiet voice on the other end.

"Mo...Mommy?"

"Amber? Sweetie? Oh, God, I'm so sorry. Mommy thought you were someone else." Jessie tried not to cry because Amber's hesitant tone showed how afraid she was. "Are you having fun at Disney?"

"Yes." Apparently that was all Amber wanted to say, because Jessie's mother came on the line.

"Jessica? I don't know what's wrong with her," Donna Greenfield said. "She was so excited to call you, and now she won't talk."

"Mom, I thought it was Wayne. I'd just hung up on him when you called. Please make sure she knows I wasn't yelling at her."

"Is he harassing you again?"

"I can handle it, Mom." Jessie sighed and got up to get a glass of orange juice.

"I don't doubt you can, but if he's bothering you, maybe you should go stay with your sister and Sarah for a few days."

"He's in Nevada." Jessie was gratified that her mother would suggest she visit her lesbian sister and her lover. Before their father died about a year ago, Donna Greenfield would never have done that. "Tell Amber I love her, and I can't wait for you guys to get home. And tell her that she better kiss Minnie for me."

They said their good-byes, and Jessie turned off the phone's ringer before she stretched out on the couch. She picked up the book and opened it to page one, noting that Lynn wouldn't be there for a couple of hours.

❖

Jessie jerked awake, insistent bells startling her. She started to shut off the alarm clock, but soon recognized the sound for what it was. Her book had fallen to the floor, so she picked it up, hastily setting it on the coffee table before she went to the front door. It had to be Lynn, because it was exactly five minutes after one.

"Hey." Lynn couldn't hide her nervousness, and Jessie wanted nothing more than to pull her into an embrace.

"Is it lunchtime already?" Jessie stepped aside, then closed the door behind her before following Lynn into the kitchen.

"Oh, please, you know I'm late. You were probably pacing in front of the door wondering where the hell I was."

"You're always late," Jessie said. Their familiar banter helped her relax. "I wouldn't know how to react if you showed up on time."

"We won't have to worry about that then, will we?" Lynn nudged her with an elbow, but then looked horrified. Jessie took her hand and led her out to the couch. After they'd both taken a seat, Lynn finally said, "I'm sorry about last night, Jessie."

"Sorry? Why?" Jessie saw the uncertainty in Lynn's eyes. "I'm not sorry about any of it. Besides, I was the one who kissed you. You have absolutely nothing to apologize for." In fact, Jessie wanted to kiss Lynn again, but something was in the way. It was Wayne. Until he was completely out of her life, she'd never be able to give herself to someone else, no matter who it was. "I also want to thank you for being the voice of reason and suggesting we sleep it off."

"You don't have to thank me." Lynn looked at their hands briefly before her eyes rested on the book on the coffee table. "I don't want to be anyone's morning-after regret."

Jessie's heart sank at the detached nonchalance in Lynn's tone. "Lynn—"

"When did you start reading lesbian romance?" Lynn picked up the book and looked at Jessie with one eyebrow raised. "You told me you'd probably never read any of my books, but here you are, presumably doing just that. Assuming, of course, this isn't Wayne's choice of reading material."

Jessie snorted. "It wouldn't surprise me if it was."

"I don't want to even consider that scenario." Lynn smiled, an obvious attempt to lighten the mood, but then her expression turned serious again. She looked back at the book she held. "When did you start reading this?"

"When I was in the hospital, the woman I shared the room with gave me a couple of books to read." Jessie sucked in a breath, wanting to take the words back as soon as they left her mouth. But Lynn didn't seem surprised. "You knew?"

"That you were in the hospital? My mother told me last night." Lynn shrugged, but Jessie saw the flash of fierce protectiveness in her eyes, quickly replaced by hurt. "Why would you keep that from me, Jess? I could have been here for you."

"You would have gone after him." And then she'd have been in prison.

"I told you I never liked him. I never trusted him. He always had that same vacant look in his eyes that your father did the day he hit me."

"Wayne didn't like you much either, but you already knew that," Jessie said with a sigh. The truth was going to come out, and she suddenly regretted not being honest with Lynn from the beginning. "He told me he was convinced you were after me—that you wanted to take me away from him. It didn't matter what I said, because he was determined to believe what he wanted to. He was jealous of the time you and I spent together around the holidays. My denials only fueled his anger."

Lynn stared at her, and Jessie wished that she would say something—anything.

"So it's my fault that he did this to you."

"Lynn, it's not your fault, any more than it's mine." Jessie had spent many nights lying awake thinking about this, both as a child with her father and now as an adult, with Wayne. The patterns were frighteningly similar. "An abuser doesn't need a valid excuse to do what they do. They constantly try to rationalize the behavior. If he hadn't been jealous over my friendship with you, he'd have found something else."

"I'm so happy you're actually divorcing him, instead of staying with him out of some warped sense of commitment." Lynn sat back again and sighed.

"I'm done with him. I told you that last night." Jessie didn't pull away when Lynn covered her hand with one of her own. Jessie was certain a spark of electricity passed between them. She met Lynn's eyes and was seriously thinking about kissing her when Lynn broke the spell.

"You wanted me to stay the night last night. Have you ever been with a woman before?"

"I'd never kissed a woman before last night." Jessie felt the corners of her mouth pulling up when Lynn released her hand. "Well, except for that once."

"God, that was awful, wasn't it?" They both laughed at the memory neither of them had ever acknowledged before, and some of Jessie's tension melted away. Lynn seemed a little more relaxed too. "I have to say—you've certainly improved as a kisser."

"Me? I was thinking you'd improved." Jessie felt her cheeks flush, but she refused to look away from Lynn.

"I'd never kissed anyone before that," Lynn said. "You shocked the hell out of me."

"I shocked the hell out of myself."

"Way back when, or last night?"

"Both." They fell quiet, and Lynn studied her hands again. So she had been Lynn's first kiss too. Jessie's heart swelled. "We should eat before that wonderful food gets cold."

"Jess, Charlie's birthday is tomorrow, and my parents are taking him out to dinner. Will you come with us?" Jessie stared at her for a moment, but Lynn refused to look up from her hands.

"Are you asking me on a date?"

"I hadn't intended for it to be that. Just two friends having dinner," Lynn said, sounding sad. Lynn finally turned her head to look at her again, uncertainty in those beautiful blue eyes. Jessie so wanted to purge it from her, but wasn't sure if she could. "The reservations are for seven."

"Then you can pick me up at six."

CHAPTER SEVEN

L ynn pulled into Jessie's driveway at five minutes after six the next evening. No matter what time she left, she always arrived five minutes late. She was glad Jessie actually expected her to do it.

She stopped at the steps to the front door. How the hell was she supposed to act? Why had Jessie asked if this was a date? Did she want it to be one? Lynn sat down on the stoop and stared out at the darkened street.

She didn't really think Jessie would use her, but what if she saw Lynn as a way to get away from Wayne once and for all? Or maybe she wanted to experiment to see if she really was attracted to women? Fuck. If this was the baggage that went along with being in love, no wonder she'd stayed away from it for so long. Maybe if she let Jessie make the first move, she could relax and just let whatever would happen, happen. Maybe. Or maybe it would all blow up in her face and she'd lose the one woman she'd loved all her life. Fuck.

"Are you planning to sit out there all evening, or would you like to come inside?"

Lynn jumped to her feet at the sound of Jessie's voice behind her. "Jesus Christ," she said as she bent over at the waist attempting to catch her breath. "You scared the hell out of me."

"I do that a lot, don't I? Come inside and have a drink."

Lynn took in Jessie's tight-fitting blue dress and hoped to God she was managing not to drool all over herself. She tried to keep her eyes averted from the plunging neckline.

"You look beautiful," she finally managed to say once they were in the kitchen.

"Thank you." Jessie blushed slightly as she smiled, and Lynn smiled back. She held her breath as Jessie gave her a thorough inspection. "You look quite nice yourself."

"Thank you." Lynn glanced down at her black slacks, green sweater, and black leather jacket. She'd put on so many outfits she'd made herself sick from indecision. She finally settled on the first thing she'd tried on. Jessie was looking at her, but she was afraid to meet her eyes. This was ridiculous. She'd never been nervous around a woman. She accepted the beer Jessie offered and took a swig before stealing another look at the revealing blue dress.

"Shouldn't I be the one who's a little on edge?" Jessie finally asked. "Because I can't help feeling like this is a date."

"You'd think so, wouldn't you?" Lynn chuckled uneasily, trying to quell her panic. "I'm not sure how to act around you anymore."

She hadn't really intended to say the words out loud, and she watched Jessie anxiously. Jessie placed her beer on the counter before taking the three steps to close the distance between them. Lynn didn't stop her when Jessie took her beer from her and set it aside. She watched quietly as Jessie touched her wrist, then slowly moved her hand up Lynn's arm, holding her gaze the entire time.

"Jess—"

"Shhh." Jessie held a finger to her lips. Lynn's legs almost gave out. "You're going to end up making *me* nervous, Lynn. I need you to relax, okay?"

Lynn nodded, marveling at the sensation of Jessie's finger on her lips. She wanted nothing more than to suck it into her mouth. Her body rebelled at her self-imposed restraint because *she* wanted to be in control, wanted to take Jessie with the abandon she'd enjoyed with other women, wanted...everything. When Jessie cupped Lynn's cheek, she was certain that Jessie was about to kiss her. After a moment, Jessie's hand slid around to the back of Lynn's neck and pulled her closer.

As soon as Jessie's mouth covered hers, Lynn's instincts took over. Jessie's hands were in her hair, urging her closer still, and when their tongues met, Lynn found Jessie's hips and pulled her tight against her body. With heels, Jessie was a couple of inches taller than Lynn. In her bare feet like she was now, Jessie was only a fraction of an inch shorter. Lynn moved her hands up the back of Jessie's dress, searching for the zipper, but Jessie pushed her away.

"Lynn, stop," she said breathlessly. Lynn eased back, and Jessie rested her forehead on her shoulder. "I'm sorry. All of this is so new to me. I need to go slow. Is that okay?"

"Yes," Lynn managed to whisper as she closed her eyes, still holding Jessie to her. "But for future reference, this is *not* the way to help me relax."

"I'm sorry."

"You don't have anything to apologize for." Lynn moved her hands to Jessie's upper arms and held her a few inches away so she could look at her face. "I'm going to let you set the pace, all right? I won't pressure you into anything. If this is going to happen, it'll be when you're comfortable with it, because like I already said, I don't want to be anybody's morning-after regret. Especially not yours. And I don't want to have regrets either, Jess."

Jessie gave her a chaste kiss on the lips. "Thank you. We should probably get going if we intend to make it to the restaurant on time."

Lynn stood there for a moment while Jessie went to get her coat and willed the blood pulsing between her legs to begin flowing somewhere else, anywhere else. Like to her brain.

This was going to be a long night.

"Jessie!" Rose exclaimed when she and Lynn walked into the waiting area. Rose stood and pulled Jessie into a warm embrace, winking over Jessie's shoulder at Lynn. "Our table should be ready in a few minutes. I was so happy when Lynn told me you'd be joining us."

Lynn rolled her eyes just as someone slapped her back. She stumbled forward and turned to see her brother standing behind her with a huge grin.

"What's up, Chuck?" she asked with a grin of her own. She laughed when his expression changed to irritation.

"I wish you wouldn't call me that."

"I know." She hugged him briefly, then stepped away. "And if you'd just ignore it instead of complaining every time, I'd probably stop doing it. Happy birthday, Charlie."

"Thanks." He smiled again when Rose finally let go of Jessie and held out his arms to greet her. "I'm glad you could join us."

"Me too, and happy birthday," Jessie said as she pulled away from him.

"Where's Dad?" Lynn asked, glancing around the immediate area.

"Still at work, but he'll be here as soon as he can." Her mother motioned for Jessie to sit next to her.

Charlie grabbed Lynn's arm and turned away from them. "We'll go get some drinks," he said over his shoulder while they walked toward the bar. When they'd given their order to the bartender, Charlie nudged Lynn with an elbow. "So, was I right? Are they separated and headed for divorce?"

"Why don't you ask her for yourself?" Lynn shook her head in annoyance. He was worse than any gossip she'd ever known.

"Maybe I should ask her out on a date," he said with a wink. "What do you think?"

Lynn stared at him for a moment, fighting the urge to punch him, then returned her attention to the bartender, who was a rather nice-looking young woman. Charlie was the only family member who'd known since high school how Lynn felt about Jessie, so he'd never really date her. Then again, how could he possibly know that Jessie was actually considering Lynn as a lover? She decided to play with him a bit.

"Maybe you should."

"Seriously? You wouldn't castrate me?"

"Why would I?" Lynn shrugged and continued to watch the woman fixing their drinks. "You know I'm a pussycat. I'd never hurt anyone if I could help it."

"Oh, I don't know—maybe because *you're* interested in her?"

"She can go out with whoever she wants, Charlie." Lynn finally turned to look at him. "I can't stop her from dating. I won't deny that I'm interested, but I can't do anything about it if *she's* not interested in me. After all, she hasn't been up to this point."

"Have you told her?"

"Here you go," the bartender said, smiling suggestively at Lynn. When Lynn held out her credit card, the woman took it, brushing Lynn's fingers with her own.

"Jesus, you do better with women than I do," Charlie grumbled.

"I always have, little bro. Stick with me, and I'll teach you everything I know." Lynn winked at the bartender before pocketing her credit card. She turned and walked back to where they had left Jessie and their mother, but she faltered. Jessie stood by the door talking to an attractive man. Lynn tried not to let her jealousy show when she sat down next to her mother. "Who's that?"

"I don't know." Rose shrugged, but was watching them just as intently as Lynn. "He came and said hello to her, and then they went over there to talk."

Lynn watched them for a moment, but then the hostess called their name. Rose and Charlie followed her to their table, but Lynn sat there a moment longer and Jessie put up a finger to indicate she'd be along in a minute. Lynn glared at the man she was talking to before getting up and trailing her mother and brother, insecurity suddenly twisting her insides into knots.

❖

When they finally left the restaurant, Jessie suggested that they go to Sarah's bar for a drink. Lynn's family declined, and obviously Lynn didn't really want to go, but she agreed to anyway. Lynn had been unusually quiet all through dinner, and Jessie couldn't get her to talk in the car either. By the time they walked into the bar, Jessie was tempted to ask Lynn to just take her home.

"Hi, ladies," Sarah said when they ordered their drinks. "Lynn, I'm glad you're here. I want to talk to you about something."

"Sure."

"Bobby, take over for a minute," Sarah told the young man working the bar with her. "I'll be back in a few minutes."

They followed Sarah into the office, which was quieter than out by the dance floor. She motioned for them to sit, then perched on the edge of her desk, a flyer in her hand.

"What's up?" Lynn asked. She took the flyer that Sarah held out, and Jessie peeked at it over Lynn's shoulder. Lynn shook her head as she handed it back. "No. I'm not interested."

It was an advertisement for an auction the bar was hosting to raise money for breast cancer research. Jessie glanced at Sarah, raising an eyebrow. Was she really asking Lynn to auction herself off for charity?

"Why? It's for a good cause, and you get a free night out on the town."

"I'm not doing it." Lynn crossed her arms over her chest. "I have no desire to go out on a date with someone I would have zero interest in."

"It's for a good cause," Sarah repeated. "I bet you'll bring in more money than anyone else. Most of the women here don't know you personally since you live in San Francisco now, and they'll start drooling as soon as you walk on stage, especially since you're a famous author. It's for a good cause."

"You've mentioned that. Repeatedly. My answer is still no."

"I think you should do it." Jessie met Lynn's incredulous stare and shrugged. If it was possible, she thought Lynn looked even more annoyed than she had during dinner. "If you can bring in a lot of money, it could only be a good thing, right?"

Lynn continued to stare at her, and Jessie was becoming uncomfortable under the scrutiny. After a moment, Lynn returned her attention to Sarah.

"Fine." Lynn stood and started toward the door. "You have my cell number. Let me know what I need to do."

"What's with her?" Sarah asked when Lynn had gone.

"I kissed her."

"Was it better this time?" Jessie was surprised that the declaration didn't seem to faze Sarah.

"Much better." Jessie laughed at Sarah's inquisitiveness, but quickly returned to the current problem. "I don't know what's wrong with her now, though."

"Honey, if you're going to be a lesbian, you need to get used to the drama. Unfortunately, it's a prerequisite. You've been in this place enough to witness some of it firsthand."

Sarah laughed, but Jessie was sure she was pulling her leg. "I need to go talk to her. Was she moody like this when you were with her?"

"She wasn't in love with me, Jess." Sarah shook her head. "She's never been in love with anyone but you."

Jessie didn't know what to say. Was it possible Lynn could be in love with her? Why hadn't she ever told her?

A wave of sadness suddenly engulfed Jessie when she thought about Lynn holding on to those feelings for so long. No wonder Lynn had refused to stay with her while she was in town. If what Sarah said was true, Jessie was determined to get Lynn to admit it.

CHAPTER EIGHT

"Have you ever been in love?" Jessie asked when Lynn pulled into her driveway a short time later. She waited for Lynn to put the car in Park, then turned off the ignition herself.

"What kind of question is that?" Lynn knew her defensiveness showed in her tone, but she didn't care. She was so conflicted she wasn't sure which way to turn.

"A simple one. I want to know if you've ever been in love. Sarah said you weren't in love with her—that you've never been in love with anyone but me. Is that true?"

"Sarah needs to mind her own damn business."

"Jesus, Lynn, just answer the question."

Lynn stared straight ahead, her throat constricted. She clenched her teeth and the muscles in her jaw jumped. This was new. Why the hell did she feel like she was about to burst into tears?

"Do we need to play true confessions?" Jessie asked after a lengthy silence. Her voice had softened, though, and Jessie could apparently tell just how close she was to breaking down.

"No. I've never been in love with anyone but you. I've never let anyone close enough. I've always held on to the fantasy that I might be with you someday. You broke my heart when you married Wayne, Jessie. Then you had a baby. God, I was devastated, because I thought you'd be with Wayne forever. A baby makes things more real, more permanent, you know?" Lynn was babbling, but if she stopped, she'd never finish. "Most people would have moved on at that point, but I must be a masochist, because I kept hoping. Then I saw Amber for the first time, and I fell in love with her too. I melt every time she calls me Auntie Lynn and gives me a big hug."

"Why didn't you ever tell me these things?" Jessie took Lynn's hand, moving it into her own lap.

"What would have been the point, Jess? I mean, seriously— you probably would have freaked out, and I might never have heard from you again." Lynn finally turned to meet Jessie's eyes, afraid she'd get lost in the depths of chocolate brown. "That would have killed me. I'd rather have you in my life as a friend than to lose you forever because you couldn't deal with how I felt, how I *feel* about you. What if I never hear from you again? What if you break my heart again, this time not because of some guy, but because you don't want *me*?"

"I can't imagine ever having you gone from my life. I don't know how I'd have reacted if you'd told me before, but we'd have remained close. You're my best friend, and I don't want that to ever change."

They sat quietly for a few moments, and Lynn allowed Jessie to intertwine their fingers, enjoying the feel of her hand. Everything about the situation was totally new to her. With anyone else, she'd be saying what her date wanted to hear, trying to get her into bed. But with Jessie, she didn't have a clue what to talk about because she was so afraid of saying the wrong thing.

"Will you come inside?" Jessie asked quietly.

"No, not tonight." Lynn slowly pulled her hand away and rubbed her palms on her slacks. "My parents' anniversary is next Wednesday. Will you come to the party? It's their fortieth."

"I can't. I have plans that evening," Jessie said.

Lynn thought she detected a hint of regret in Jessie's tone and tried to not let her disappointment show.

"Does that mean I won't be seeing you before then?"

Lynn shrugged. "That's up to you."

"What happened between the time we left here and the time we were seated in the restaurant?" Jessie's irritated tone was back, and Lynn wanted to tell her, but couldn't bear to lay her feelings out any more than she already had.

"Nothing. I've just been thinking about things. I know this is all new to you, Jessie, and I understand that you need some time to wrap your head around it. It would probably be easier for you if I wasn't hanging around here every day."

The hurt she saw in Jessie's eyes almost made her give in. Then she remembered how overly familiar Jessie had been acting with the man in the restaurant. "Jess, I don't want to be an experiment. Until two days ago, you never questioned that you were straight. How do I know you don't see this as an easy way to get Wayne out of your life forever? Just a temporary replacement, you know?"

She regretted the words as soon as they left her mouth but couldn't take them back. She held Jessie's gaze and braced herself for the anger flashing in her eyes.

"How dare you." Jessie reached for the door handle. "I thought we knew each other too well for bullshit like this. Obviously I was wrong. And you have absolutely no idea what was going through my mind until two days ago. I care about you, Lynn, but clearly I need to give this"—she pointed back and forth between the two of them—"much more consideration than I originally thought. I'll call you."

She rocketed out of the car and slammed the door behind her. Lynn bent forward and rested her head on the steering wheel, fighting the urge to run after her.

Communication had never been one of her strong points. Why hadn't Jessie refuted the possibility that she might be an experiment? Damn. She might have just fucked up the most important relationship in her life.

Jessie stood with her back against the door until Lynn drove away almost five minutes later. Then she hung her head and began to cry softly. Her purse fell to the floor and she followed, slowly sliding down until she slumped fully to the floor. She hadn't intended for the evening to end this way. She'd never wanted anyone more than she wanted Lynn, and the depth of that desire terrified her.

Using her to get away from Wayne—what a crock. If Wayne had a clue what was happening between them, he'd probably come after them both. She stopped crying and whipped her head up, slamming it against the door with a thud.

"Maybe this is for the best," she said to the dark hallway, but her words didn't keep her from reliving the scene in the kitchen before they'd left for dinner. The feel of Lynn's body against hers had ignited a fire in her that wouldn't be easy to put out. Jessie had never imagined that another woman could arouse these feelings in her. She reached in her purse for a tissue and felt the cold steel of the gun. She pulled it out, then clicked on the light in the entryway.

When Rick Tompkins, her attorney, had first suggested she get a gun, she laughed at him. As more time went by, though, she considered what Wayne had done and what he could still do. She'd finally given in a couple of months ago, and Rick had taken her to the shooting range a few times. Even though she abhorred the thought of using the .38 against another human being, she actually enjoyed the practice and was even quite good. Since she had proved herself on the shooting range and had no prior run-ins with the law, she easily got a license to carry a concealed weapon. If Wayne ever showed up on her doorstep, she'd be able to defend herself. And her child.

But what about Lynn? If Wayne did catch wind of something between them, would she stand a chance if he decided to go after her? A chill raced down her spine. She shook her head and replaced the gun in her purse. No, it was probably best that their romance stop before it got a chance to develop. She wished, not for the first time, that Wayne was dead. She'd never have a normal life as long as he was around.

That was probably better for Lynn too. What exactly did Lynn want from her? Sarah had said that while Lynn had been faithful to her when they were together, she tended to sleep around when she was single, and Lynn had never denied that fact. She seemed to enjoy her lifestyle, and having a girlfriend with a young child would certainly put a damper on that. What if she only wanted a fling? She was returning to San Francisco at the end of the month, after all, and presumably wouldn't be back until the following December. How would a relationship like that work?

Jessie sighed as she stood and removed her coat. Why couldn't life ever give her easy choices?

"It's for the best," she said with more resolve than she felt. Maybe if she repeated it enough times, she'd start to believe it.

CHAPTER NINE

L ynn walked into The Family Room Sunday evening where Sarah sat at a table in the corner, a cup of coffee in front of her and a pen in her hand. Lynn took a seat at the table without asking if she could.

"You're enemy number one at the moment." Sarah didn't look up from her paperwork.

"Excuse me?"

Sarah put down the pen and stared at her as she removed her reading glasses. Before she spoke again, she waved to the bartender for a refill.

"Karen's not happy with you, and neither am I. Jessie and Karen had dinner last night, and Jess told Karen what you said." Sarah sat back in her seat and folded her arms. "That was so not cool, dude. About her using you to get away from Wayne? Not cool at all. That doesn't sound like the Lynn Patrick I used to know."

Lynn had expected the recrimination but had no idea what to say. She'd felt bad about it even before Jessie had disappeared into the house Friday night, and she'd seriously considered knocking on the door to apologize. In the end, she'd finally driven away and fought the urge to call Jessie ever since. She was starting to worry that she might never hear from Jessie again, but she didn't want to be the one to cave in first. What if Jessie *didn't* want to talk to her? In some way, it was better not to know. Even if it was killing her.

"I know. I'm a shit. What can I say?"

"Well, to start with, you could apologize to her."

"When she got out of the car, she told me that *she'd* call *me*. I don't think she wants to hear from me right now."

"She'd love to hear that you didn't mean it. You *didn't* mean it, did you?"

"Of course not." Lynn shook her head at the bartender when he came to fill Sarah's cup, indicating that she didn't want anything. She was on her way to Charlie's for dinner and didn't want to show up drunk. They were finally planning to have that talk about his failed marriage.

She rested her forearms on the table and met Sarah's fiery gaze. "Well, maybe. I said it in the heat of the moment. After that I realized she could easily find another man and stick to safer relationships. But what if she does want someone safe? Someone totally different from Wayne, and for the moment that's me? I can't live my life wondering if the woman I love would rather be with a man. And, yeah, maybe the way I said it and the timing weren't great, but I still wonder if it might be true."

"I don't understand you. You've always wanted Jessie to wake up one day and realize that she loves you. Now that it's a real possibility, you're doing everything you can to sabotage it before it can get going. You know Jessie better than anyone. Do you honestly think she'd do that?"

"No," Lynn finally said. Sighing, she ran both hands through her hair. "Fuck, Sarah, I'm scared. I don't want this to be a transitional relationship for her. I don't want to find out that she's only considering turning to women because she's disenchanted with men. Somebody who's straight doesn't suddenly find herself attracted to women. I don't think Jessie would do it intentionally, but she's a mess right now and has a shitload of crap going on in her life. She might do it without even realizing, then suddenly she wakes up one day and wonders what the hell she was thinking, wanting to be with a woman."

"Ah, and there we have the crux of the problem," Sarah said with a nod. "Honey, you need to sit down and have a serious conversation with her. This attraction didn't suddenly happen when you confessed your love. I've been noticing it in her for months, and honestly, Karen said it's been longer than that. You're the only person who seems surprised."

Lynn sat there stunned while Sarah went to help a customer at the bar. Was it true? If Jessie had been considering being with women for some time now, who was the guy she was talking to at the restaurant the other night? Maybe she was bisexual, and while that never held much appeal for Lynn in a partner, it seemed to be different where Jessie was concerned. *Everything* seemed to be different where Jessie was concerned, and that fact bothered her. Suddenly nothing in her world made sense, which was pissing her off.

Lynn snapped back to the present when Sarah set a shot glass filled with whiskey and a beer in front of her. Every bartender she was familiar with seemed to know exactly what she wanted. She was about to drink the shot when someone smacked the back of her head, hard. She stood and turned to meet Karen Greenfield's eyes.

"What the fuck's wrong with you?" Karen asked in lieu of a greeting.

"It's nice to see you too," Lynn responded, rubbing the back of her head. She took her seat again as Karen pulled a chair over from an adjacent table. Lynn marveled, as she always did, at how much Karen and Jessie looked alike. They had the same brown eyes and hair, but Karen was a couple inches shorter than Jessie, and only Jessie shared Lynn's passion for ice hockey.

"You hurt my sister," Karen said when she was settled. "What are you going to do about it?"

"Maybe if you'd have cuffed Wayne like that he wouldn't have hit Jessie." Lynn grimaced, knowing she sounded judgmental and petulant, but not giving a damn. Karen, however, took the statement and ran with it.

"Don't even get me started on that piece of shit. Leave me alone with him for thirty seconds, and I'll castrate him. That poor excuse for a human being deserves to live the rest of his life without his manhood, and maybe spend a little time in jail without it. Then perhaps he'd see what it felt like to have someone beat the shit out of him."

"Amen," Sarah said, then the three of them hushed. Lynn presumed they were all thinking about ways to make Wayne Paulson suffer.

"You didn't answer my question," Karen eventually said, her tone a bit more amiable. Lynn finally swallowed her shot and met Karen's stare.

"I'm going to apologize to her."

"Tonight?"

"I'm having dinner with Charlie tonight." She wanted to blow him off and rush right over to Jessie's house, but while he would understand, she wanted to keep her commitment. She wouldn't be able to see Jessie until at least tomorrow.

"If she comes crying to me again, I'll hunt you down, Patrick." Karen meant it. Though she acted feminine, her heart was pure butch. "I want to hear from her that you called and apologized, understood? You two have been friends far too long to let some bullshit like this come between you."

"I got it." Lynn nodded. She'd better do it soon. She should have expected this, because Jessie had always told Karen everything, probably even how she felt about Lynn, but she wasn't about to ask. "You don't seem to be surprised that your sister might be gay."

"Oh, please, I knew it was only a matter of time." Karen shrugged. "Honestly, I'm only worried about how our mother reacts to the news. I'm just glad Jessie waited to realize this until after our father died, because Mom's a lot more accepting of me now. I'm sure she will be about Jessie too, if it turns out that she is a lesbian. Especially since Mom's already gotten the grandchild she wanted so badly."

They all fell quiet again, and Lynn fought to sit still under their intense study.

"What exactly did Wayne do to her?" Lynn finally asked the one question she'd wanted to ask Jessie since she'd first learned about the abuse. "How long was she in the hospital?"

Karen glanced at Sarah and shifted in her seat, peeling the label from her beer.

"Just over a week. As far as her injuries, you'd better ask her."

"Why didn't somebody call me?"

"Jessie didn't want you to know," Sarah said, echoing Lynn's mother's statement. She was getting annoyed that nobody thought she could offer comfort and be there for her friend. "I didn't understand it at the time, but the other night she finally told me about the time you threatened their father."

"That bastard gave me one hell of a shiner." Lynn grinned, and soon they were all laughing.

"God, I wish I could have seen it," Karen said. "You were Jessie's own personal hero after that. I never thanked you for what you did that day. You know, he never touched her again after your little talk with him. I think you scared the bejeezus out of him. So, thank you. You did what I was never able to."

"You're welcome, but I'm not sure I'd have done it if I'd had time to think. It all happened so fast." Lynn finished her beer and looked at her watch. "I better get going. Charlie's expecting me in about five minutes, and I can't possibly make it there in that time."

"Don't forget about the auction Friday night," Sarah said as Lynn stood.

"She's in it?" Karen asked. "Cool. We'll make a bundle to save the boobies."

"Shit, that's the whole reason I came in here tonight. What do I have to do?"

"Just be yourself. You could wear a tux if you feel so moved." Sarah took Karen's hand. "Be here by six thirty, because we start promptly at seven."

"And what does the high bidder get? I'm not selling my soul here, am I?"

"I told you. A date with you, stud," Sarah said, and Karen laughed. "Just dinner, and whatever else you decide you're willing to give up for the winner."

"I'm thinking it's going to be just dinner." Lynn winked as she zipped up her jacket and left the bar.

CHAPTER TEN

L ynn was surprised when she got to Charlie's house and was greeted at the door by her young niece and nephew. Obviously their mother had no idea Lynn was having dinner with them, because if she had, she wouldn't have allowed the children to stay. Lynn glanced at Charlie questioningly, and he simply laughed when the kids assaulted her before she could even get her jacket off.

"I think they were starting to believe you were Santa Claus," he said after he'd sent them off to the living room and he and Lynn went to the kitchen. "The only time they ever saw you was on Christmas Eve."

"We can thank Witch Ellen for that," Lynn replied, not trying to hide her distaste. "I thought you said she took the kids and moved home."

"She did." Charlie nodded before he took the pizza out of the oven. At Lynn's look of amusement, he shrugged. "I know I said we'd have steak, but the kids insisted on pizza. Next time, I promise."

"I won't hold my breath."

"Anyway, her mother lives in Gresham instead of Seattle now, which is nice because I get to see my kids more often, but it sure sucks to have her so near." Charlie set the pizza on the counter and began cutting it as he talked. "She decided that since it was my birthday Friday, I should get the kids for the weekend. She dropped them off yesterday morning, and I have to take them to school tomorrow. I won't see them again until Christmas Eve."

"I know you're dying to tell me, so what happened?" Lynn waited as he held a finger up and called the kids in to get their dinner. When their plates were full, he settled them at the coffee table, then returned to the kitchen.

"She started seeing someone else," Charlie finally said as he sat across the table from her. He bit into a slice of pizza and watched her intently, apparently waiting for some kind of smart remark. She vowed to keep the snide comments to herself—at least for the moment.

"Just like that?"

"Evidently they'd been seeing each other for quite some time." Charlie took a drink of his beer and sat back in his chair. "I only found out about it because I was sick one day and came home from work early. She had her little boy toy here that day."

"Were they—"

"In my bed, thrashing around like wild animals. I was so shocked, I just stood there for a couple of minutes, not knowing what to say. They were so involved in what they were doing they didn't even notice me there at the foot of the bed."

"I bet you were pissed." Lynn was trying to look serious and hoped she was pulling it off. She couldn't imagine what Charlie had gone through, and she was sure he didn't need her rubbing it in all over again, no matter how much she disliked his wife. Charlie nodded and sighed.

"Once I calmed down, I was oddly at peace. I grabbed him and threw him out the front door without his clothes. God, this all sounds like a bad cliché, doesn't it?" He laughed and Lynn joined him. "I decided to let *her* get dressed before I began pitching all her things out on the front lawn. I filed for divorce the next morning."

"So why did she take the kids?"

"I decided to be diplomatic about it, for now anyway. I figured it might help me when she tries to sue for sole custody."

"And you know damn well Witch Ellen will." They picked up their beers and clinked them together before drinking.

As they continued eating, Lynn wondered if Charlie was as upset about the end of his marriage as she'd first thought. He didn't seem to be hurting much, and she hoped she was right about that. For a while they left the subject alone and talked about life in general, catching up and laughing the way they had before she moved to California.

"I know you've been dying to say it, so get it over with, will you?" Charlie finally said after they'd cleaned up and the kids were in bed. They were sitting in the living room, each with a fresh beer, and had exhausted all of the small talk Lynn could handle for one evening.

"What? I told you so?" Lynn nudged him with an elbow. "I won't say that, Charlie. I know you loved her and I was always against her—for very good reasons, I might add. I never thought anything like this would happen, though."

"In a way, I'm glad it did." He smiled a bit sheepishly. "I've met someone too."

"I hope she's more tolerant of your lesbian sister than Ellen was."

"She has quite a few gay friends, so I'm sure she'll be fine with it. I haven't talked about you yet, though—talking about my sister on a date seems a little weird."

"Trust me, Chuckie, I never talk about you when I'm with a woman either."

"I guess that would kind of put a damper on things for you, huh?"

"So...were you having an affair too?" Lynn asked carefully after a few moments.

"No," he answered with a laugh. "I actually haven't slept with her yet. We've only known each other about a month, and an occasional lunch is all we've shared so far. What about you, big sister? Anyone in your life that's important enough for more than a one-night stand?"

Lynn shook her head but couldn't help laughing. Charlie had always encouraged her to tell Jessie how she felt, but he—like Bri— always figured she'd never actually do it.

"I told Jessie that I love her."

His face registered surprise, then a huge grin formed. "It's about fucking time. But what about Wayne? Are they separated?"

"Yes, and heading for divorce. The bastard was turning into her father." Lynn fought to keep from clenching her fists. Every time she thought about what he'd done, anger welled up inside her.

"He beat her?" Charlie was stunned, which surprised Lynn. She'd assumed everyone except her had known. *They knew he'd tell me.* She and Charlie had always been close, so clearly they'd kept the knowledge from him as well. His jaw muscles tightened, a family trait they shared. "I really hated Arthur Greenfield. I never understood how any man could do to a woman what he did to his wife and daughters. I know I shouldn't feel this way, but I was actually relieved when I heard that he died. I was glad Karen and Jessie would never have to deal with him again. He was a bad, bad man, Lynn. Wayne did the same thing?"

Lynn nodded and they sat there until Charlie apparently couldn't contain his curiosity any longer.

"So when did you finally tell her?"

"Friday night, after dinner."

"Why didn't you let me know before now?"

"It doesn't matter, because I haven't seen or talked to her since I dropped her off that night."

"Why? What happened?"

"I let my insecurities show. I insinuated that I thought she might be using me to get rid of Wayne once and for all."

"That was stupid."

"Gee, thanks." Lynn placed her bottle on the end table and looked up at the ceiling. "She ripped into me, and I haven't heard from her since."

"Wait a minute. This is because of that guy she was talking to at the restaurant, isn't it? Lynn, just because she *talks* to a man doesn't mean she wants to *be* with him."

"But what if she's only considering women because she's had bad male role models?" Lynn asked quietly. "What if she finds a man who'll treat her the way she deserves to be treated? Where will that leave me?"

"Jesus, Lynn. She might be gay because men abused her? I know you realize how stupid that sounds. Some people who were abused are gay, and others are straight. Just like some abused people turn out to be serial killers, and others go on to lead completely normal lives. Who can really say whether or not the abuse has anything to do with any of it? I know Jessie, and so do you. If she *is* a lesbian, it's because of what's in her heart, not because of something that Wayne and her father did to her. You should maybe think about something, though, sis. Perhaps she isn't considering *women*. Maybe she's just considering *you*."

Sometime during Charlie's little soapbox speech, Lynn really looked at him and wondered when the hell her little brother had grown up. She grinned as she took his hand.

"Have I told you lately how proud I am to have you as a brother?"

"Now that you mention it, no." He squeezed her hand. "A few more things before I stop. If anything happens between the two of you, it'll be because she loves you, not because she thinks you can help her get out of a bad situation. And if she does love you, neither a man—or woman—will be able to turn her head. And here's the big thing—what in God's name are you doing hanging out with me when you should be with Jessie trying to make things right?"

"I can take a hint." Lynn stood to leave, Charlie following her. "I should leave anyway, because I'm not used to you saying such heartfelt things. It's going to ruin my image of you."

"Hey, I have two tickets to the Winterhawks game Friday night. You'll come with me, right?"

"I'd love to, man, but I have plans I can't get out of. I agreed to be auctioned off for charity." She laughed at his expression of shock.

"Forget the hockey game. I wouldn't miss that auction for the world."

"It's at a gay bar," she warned him, hoping to dissuade him.

He shook his head. "I don't care. I need to see this. I'll bet Mom will want to go too. Maybe even Dad. It could be a family night out."

Lynn dipped her head in defeat before she retrieved her jacket from the hall closet and put it on. She turned to say something else to him, but his expression of amusement stopped her.

Friday's definitely going to suck.

CHAPTER ELEVEN

Lynn sat in her car outside of Jessie's house. For about ten minutes, she tried to convince herself that she was doing the right thing by coming here. She really did need to apologize for the insensitive things she'd said, and it was childish to expect Jessie to be the first to call.

Maybe it was too late to just be dropping by out of the blue. A quick glance at the clock told her it wasn't even ten o'clock, and the downstairs lights were still on. Obviously, it wasn't too late.

She sighed. When the hell had she become such a ball of nerves? No one had ever affected her the way Jessie did, and she was surprised that simply because she'd spoken those words—"I've never been in love with anyone but you"—she was suddenly a totally different person. *Everything* was at stake now. This wasn't just some anonymous woman she was bringing home to spend the night. It was Jessie, and it suddenly mattered to Lynn how Jessie perceived her.

Lynn had been with enough straight women to know the dangers of getting involved, because they almost always went back to men. That had never mattered before, because Lynn had never wanted anything more than one night with them. With Jessie she wanted a lifetime—and that scared her, because what if Jessie really did end up breaking her heart? Jesus, she didn't think she could survive that. Plenty of women enjoyed being with women every once in a while, but she didn't want to be a "once in a while" for Jessie. But then, plenty of women came out late in life. Maybe she was just a late bloomer? Lynn gently banged her head against the steering wheel.

At least one of Jessie's major concerns about the two of them was most probably how Wayne would react. But what if Jessie simply didn't want a relationship with another woman? Letting her family's encouragement influence her, Lynn had allowed herself to think that the two of them had a chance, but what if—

Lynn jumped when her phone rang and ripped her out of her thoughts. She pulled it out of her jacket pocket and looked at the display, then at the house—Jessie. She was watching her through the kitchen window.

"Hi," she said, without taking her eyes from where Jessie stood.

"Do you plan to make a habit of sitting outside my house?" The tone of amusement in Jessie's voice helped Lynn relax a bit. "Because even though I think it's cute that I can make you this nervous, you're going to give me a complex. And people will think I have a stalker."

"I want to apologize for the other night."

"Come inside and have a cup of coffee."

Lynn replaced the phone in her pocket and took a long, deep breath. She wasn't thinking about any of her reservations now because all she could think about was having Jessie in her arms. And hoping to God that Jessie would forgive her.

Jessie had the door open before Lynn reached the front steps, and she walked in without a word. When Jessie shut the door, Lynn faced her.

"I'm so sorry, Jess," she said quietly, waiting for Jessie to unleash her anger again. But Jessie simply held out a hand to take her jacket.

"Thank you." Jessie hung it up, then led Lynn into the kitchen.

Jessie's calm attitude was somehow worse than if she'd let her anger and disappointment out. Lynn waited for the attitude Jessie had shown the other night to surface again. Jessica's cool indifference was killing her.

"Jess, you have to know I didn't mean what I said the other night."

"Do I?" Jessie asked. She handed Lynn a beer and sat at the

breakfast bar with her own bottle. "Lynn, I think I got so mad at you because, on some level, you might have been right."

Lynn's heart sank, but she tried hard to hide her hurt and disappointment. She'd never experienced pain like this in her chest, and she didn't like it. She didn't trust herself to speak without her voice breaking, so she waited for Jessie to go on.

"I'm struggling with this, Lynn," she finally said after an uncomfortable silence. "I'm a wife and a mother. Until a few months ago, I never even considered that I might be interested in women. But lately, it seems to be the *only* thing I can think about. When you kiss me, you make me feel like I'm the most beautiful woman in the world. I honestly don't know what'll happen between the two of us, but no matter what, I don't want to lose you as a friend. You're the most important person in my life besides Amber, and I couldn't bear it."

"You won't, Jess." Lynn's voice was tight. She put her hand over Jessie's on the counter and sighed in relief when she didn't pull away. "I don't know what'll happen between us either, but I do know this, and I told you before—I won't pressure you into anything. I can promise you that. Whatever happens—or doesn't happen—will be entirely up to you."

"Thank you," Jessie said, finally meeting her eyes, and Lynn sucked in a breath at the desire that swelled inside her. "That's a nice change of pace from what I've experienced in the past."

A burst of anger replaced the wanting, and Lynn had to turn her head so Jessie wouldn't see her hatred for Wayne expressed in her eyes. She calmed her emotions before moving her chair closer to Jessie and risked looking at her again.

Lynn touched the scar on Jessie's cheek again, and Jessie melted into the touch. "What did he do to you?" she asked softly.

Jessie had known she would have to eventually tell Lynn about that night, and now was as good a time as any. She closed her eyes and thought back to that awful experience.

Wayne had come home from work later than usual, in an extremely foul mood. He was yelling at her because he'd tripped over one of Amber's toys on his way to the living room. Amber was crying, and Jessie was scared for her. She quickly took Amber upstairs to her room and convinced her to stay there, no matter what happened. When Jessie returned to the living room, Wayne was working on his second scotch.

"Do you want me to get you something to eat?" she asked, trying to be careful not to say anything to anger him further.

Rather than speaking, he turned and backhanded her. She hadn't expected the blow, and its force knocked her to the floor. She refused to cry, because that had fueled his anger the first time. As she tried to get back to her feet, Wayne kicked her hard in the side, and she couldn't suppress the shout that escaped her when something cracked inside her.

"Shit!" he yelled, and threw his glass. The heavy leaded crystal broke against her cheek, and a warm wetness spread across her face. "Why do you make me do these things, you fucking bitch? Why do you spend all your time with those fucking dykes and make a fool out of me? I know you're sleeping with that friend of yours from San Francisco. If I ever catch the two of you together, I'll kill you both."
He stormed out of the house without another word.

Jessie stayed on the floor for a few minutes, not believing what had happened. When she was certain he wasn't coming back for another round, she slowly dragged herself to the living room. Her side hurt too much for her to attempt to get to her feet. She did manage to get the phone off the end table, called Karen, and told her what had happened right before she lost consciousness.

"So, that wasn't the first time he hit you?"

If Lynn was any angrier than she'd been before Jessie's explanation, she didn't show it. She seemed to be more concerned than anything else, and Jessie was grateful for that.

"No." Jessie was ashamed she'd gotten herself into the situation in the first place, and she looked away from Lynn, staring into her untouched coffee. "I'd always told myself I'd never get involved with a man like my father, but I certainly didn't jump to end the relationship after the first time he hit me. He apologized, and things really were better for a while. I'm still not completely sure what set him off that last time. It happened in April, and you'd been back in California almost four months, so I have no idea where he got the idea that you and I were sleeping together."

"This is from the broken glass?" Lynn again rubbed her thumb gently over the scar on her cheekbone, and Jessie closed her eyes for a moment.

"Yes. It took six stitches to close it. I also had two broken ribs, and evidently I hit my head on the corner of the counter here," she touched it to show Lynn what she was talking about, "which gave me a pretty severe concussion. But I honestly don't remember that part. I also don't remember landing so hard that I broke my collarbone *and* dislocated my shoulder. I was in the hospital for over a week."

"I wish I could have been here for you, Jess." Lynn's voice was barely audible, and she was clearly trying to hold back tears.

"I was just so scared he would hurt you," Jessie said, and she couldn't stop the sob that escaped her. She didn't resist when Lynn stood, pulled her up, and wrapped her arms around her. Jessie automatically put her arms around Lynn's waist and they held each other, her head resting on Lynn's shoulder.

"I'm here for you now, Jess, and I'll be here for as long as you want me."

CHAPTER TWELVE

"So, your brother tells us you're being auctioned off Friday," Lynn's father, Robert, said after they were seated for dinner on Wednesday night. The restaurant was quiet, and Lynn looked around to make sure no one overheard. "When were you planning to let us in on the fun?"

"I didn't think you'd be interested." Lynn looked from her father to her mother and smiled in surprise. She was happy that he wanted to know about her life, period. He usually stuck to safer topics, like sports, religion, or even politics.

"We want to be there," he told her as he opened his menu.

"We do?" Rose asked, winking in Lynn's direction.

"I know I do." Charlie sat back with a smug expression, and Lynn kicked him under the table. He rubbed his shin with a grimace. "Stop that."

"Stop fighting, you two," Robert said without looking at them. He covered his wife's hand on the table. "It's our fortieth wedding anniversary, and your mother and I won't be putting up with this crap."

Lynn stuck her tongue out at Charlie before she turned to their mother.

"It starts at seven, at The Family Room." Lynn picked up her own menu. "I'm not sure you really want to go, though. These things can get pretty crazy."

"I want to see what my daughter's worth on the open market," Rose said, grinning. "But what exactly do you mean by 'crazy'?"

"You know, girls dancing with girls, boys with boys, that kind of thing." Charlie laughed when Lynn glared at him. "You just better make sure nobody hits on me."

"Trust me, none of those boys would want to dance with you, Chuckie."

"What do you mean?" He gave Lynn the reaction she was hoping for, and she laughed. "I'm not bad-looking. Maybe I can change one of the lesbians."

"Grow up, Charlie," their father said. He lowered his menu and glared at him. "You can't change one of them any more than one of those boys could change you."

"Who are you, and what have you done with my father?" Lynn asked. Robert allowed the slightest hint of a smile before blocking his face with the menu again. Lynn glanced at her mother, but Rose was studying her own menu. The whole scenario was completely opposite from their past interactions. Usually her father never mentioned her lesbianism, like a case of don't ask, don't tell. He knew what she was, but apparently didn't want to talk about it. She suspected her mother had something to do with the sudden broadening of his mind. Lynn put down her menu and got up. "Order me a glass of merlot. I need to use the restroom."

She had to walk through the bar area to get to the ladies' room, and as she neared the end of the bar, she saw Jessie sitting alone, a glass of wine in front of her. Lynn walked up behind her and touched her elbow.

"Fancy meeting you here." She couldn't conceal her delight when Jessie turned to face her.

"Hey, you." Jessie's expression let Lynn know she was genuinely happy to see her, which caused a warm feeling in the pit of Lynn's stomach.

Lynn hadn't wanted to leave Jessie's the night she'd apologized, but she knew Jessie needed some time alone to think. Jessie was physically exhausted after telling Lynn about what Wayne had done to her, and Lynn had helped her get into bed, giving her nothing more than a chaste kiss on the cheek.

"You said you had plans tonight. I didn't know the plan was to sit alone at a bar."

"I'm not alone," Jessie said, and Lynn felt as if she'd been kicked in the stomach.

"Oh." Lynn glanced back toward her own table, and when she looked at Jessie, her attention was there as well. "Some friends of my parents wanted to throw them a surprise party. We'd planned on doing dinner here anyway, so their friends are getting the house ready now. I'm sorry I bothered you."

"Lynn, you aren't bothering me." Jessie looked confused for a moment and put a hand on Lynn's forearm. Something over her shoulder had diverted Jessie's gaze, and Lynn turned to see a man approaching. The same man Jessie had been talking to at the restaurant last Friday night. Jessie was smiling when Lynn faced her again. "I want you to meet someone."

Lynn shook her head in disbelief. Jessie wanted her to meet her date? After all they'd talked about the other night? That was a red flag if Lynn had ever seen one. Jessie obviously wasn't ready to give up the straight life yet. Could she be a bigger fool?

"Lynn Patrick, I'd like you to meet Rick Tompkins, my—"

"Nice to meet you." Lynn stuck out her hand for Rick to shake. He took it, but looked confused also as he glanced at Jessie. Lynn pulled her hand away quickly and said to her, "I should be getting back."

"Lynn, you don't have to go." Jessie stood and placed a hand on the small of her back, but Lynn pulled away feeling as if she'd been stung. "What's wrong with you?"

"I'm sorry I interrupted your date." Lynn quickly headed back to her table, forgetting that she needed to use the restroom. Her need to get away from them trumped her need to pee. Lynn had definitely never experienced jealousy before and never wanted to again.

❖

"Date?" Rick asked when Lynn was gone. He raised an eyebrow in amusement. "You told her we were on a date?"

"No, I did not." Jessie shook her head and continued to stare in disbelief at Lynn's retreating back. She finally faced forward and looked at Rick, who was standing a little taller with his chest puffed out. She slapped him playfully on the arm. "Stop it. You're like a brother to me, and I've told you that every time you've tried to get me to go out with you."

"Siblings date in some parts of the world." He shrugged before placing his forearms on the bar and wiggling his eyebrows. "You know I'm not serious about dating you, and my girlfriend would kill me anyway. You could certainly do a lot worse than me, though, Jessie. I'm a gentleman."

"Wayne was a gentleman too. At least in the beginning."

"I'm nothing like Wayne." Rick sat on the bar stool next to her and motioned for the bartender to give him a draft. "Wayne Paulson is a prick of the worst kind. He's a disgrace to men everywhere."

"I know you're nothing like him, Rick, and I'm sorry." She couldn't help but glance over her shoulder toward Lynn's table. Her heart sank when Lynn met her gaze for a moment, then turned away quickly, her eyes distant and hard.

"Oh, crap. That's *Lynn*? The Lynn you said Wayne was jealous of?"

"So what if she is?" Jessie glared at him.

Rick turned to look at Lynn again, then smiled as he faced the bar once more. "I can certainly understand his being worried. She's extremely attractive, Jessie. If my girlfriend was spending a lot of time in that woman's company, I'd be a little jealous too."

"He wasn't jealous, he was obsessed. And Lynn has been my best friend since second grade, you ass." It suddenly struck Jessie that *Lynn* was jealous. After everything they'd talked about a few nights before, she was angry that Lynn would still second-guess her intentions. She resisted the urge to twist in her seat and look at Lynn again.

"I asked you this before, Jessie, but I need to ask it again, especially after that encounter."

"No, I have not slept with her," Jessie said, forestalling his inquiry. *But I sure want to.* "After I met Wayne, I was never involved with anyone else, but we've already talked about all that."

Rick held up a hand as he reached into his pocket for his phone, which had apparently been vibrating. He turned the other way so Jessie couldn't hear his conversation, and she took the moment to study her wineglass.

The entire situation was ridiculous. If she and Lynn were ever going to have anything between them, they definitely had to communicate better. The whole jealousy thing wouldn't work, but it was flattering. She liked knowing she could elicit such strong feelings from Lynn. She looked up at Rick when he pocketed his phone.

"I need to go, but remember what I said. If Wayne causes problems for you, it'll probably be in the next few days. Be careful, and keep a lookout for him. If he's intent on seeing you, a restraining order won't do much good."

Jessie nodded and he bent down to kiss her on the cheek. She waited a few minutes after he was gone before strolling over to Lynn's table. Rose gave her a big smile when she stopped there.

"Jessie! What are you doing here?" Rose glanced at Lynn, seeming properly annoyed. "Why didn't you tell us you invited Jessie to dinner?" Rose's eyes were twinkling.

"She had other plans."

"Rose, don't bother." Jessie looked at Lynn, who finally turned her attention to her, obviously perplexed. "I planned to meet you here for dinner. Your mother asked me at Charlie's birthday dinner, because she wanted to surprise you. She seemed to think you might enjoy my company."

"I don't understand. Then what were you doing here with Rick?"

"Rick's my attorney. He's also Karen's boss and a good family friend. He called me this afternoon because he wanted to let me know that Wayne's going to be served the divorce papers tomorrow. I figured since I'd be here for dinner tonight, it would be more convenient for him to meet me here to discuss the situation."

"You're not dating him?" Lynn had gone pale. Obviously she'd realized she'd stuck her foot in her mouth once again. Jessie smiled, but wasn't quite ready to let Lynn off the hook.

"No, but perhaps I should consider it. He's asked me out often enough." Jessie waited a moment for the words to sink in, then placed a hand on Rose's shoulder. "I'm sorry, Rose, I don't think I should stay for dinner, but thank you for inviting me. Congratulations on forty wonderful years together. I hope you enjoy forty more."

She turned and walked away, but before she could make it to the front doors, Lynn was behind her, lightly gripping her elbow.

"Jessie, I'm sorry."

Jessie looked at her and motioned for Lynn to follow her outside. They walked to Jessie's car without speaking, and once they were there, Jessie faced her.

"Maybe you should think things through a little more, and then you wouldn't keep doing or saying things you need to apologize for. It's nice to know that you care so much, but I really can't deal with jealousy. I had enough of that with Wayne. I need someone who can love and trust me, Lynn. Just because I talk to a man, I'm not necessarily sleeping with him, or even *want* to sleep with him. Like I said before, I honestly don't know where this thing between us is headed, but I do know it won't go *anywhere* if you react like a sulking child every time I talk to someone else. I already have one child—I don't need to deal with two."

Without allowing Lynn time to respond, Jessie got into her car. She glanced up at Lynn before backing out of the parking space and could have sworn she saw a tear rolling down Lynn's cheek. She hoped Lynn didn't see the tear she refused to remove from her own cheek before she pulled out into traffic.

CHAPTER THIRTEEN

Surprise parties had never been one of Lynn's favorite ways to spend an evening. She stayed about ten minutes, because her mother asked her to, before deciding to go out and get a drink. She was a little taken aback to find Sarah tending bar on a Wednesday, but she couldn't deny that she was happy to see her. When they were together, Sarah had always been able to make the bleakest situation a little brighter. She desperately needed Sarah's optimism tonight.

"What are you doing here? I thought Jessie went out to dinner with you and your family tonight."

"Give me a draft." Lynn really didn't want to talk about her evening. She hated admitting to failure. "I fucked it all up again."

"What did you say this time?" Sarah set the full mug down, then poured herself a cup of coffee before settling in. Lynn told her everything that had happened at the restaurant, and Sarah listened without interrupting, but shook her head when Lynn finished. "Jesus, Patrick, when did you go and get all possessive? It isn't like you to be jealous."

"I know, right? I don't understand it. I've never felt like this before, Sarah." Lynn hung her head, resting her elbows on the bar. "I feel like I'm running in circles and can't get out of the cycle. I keep saying things I shouldn't and assuming things that I should know aren't true. What the hell's wrong with me?"

"You're in love, that's what. It can do crazy things to a person— make them do really stupid things that they wouldn't normally do."

Sarah noisily sipped her coffee, and when Lynn didn't raise her head, Sarah touched her forearm, causing Lynn to finally look up. "Jessie's going through a rough time right now, and you need to let her work through all these feelings. I know patience has never been your strong suit, but if you really want her, you need to understand she has to get rid of Wayne. He's scared the living crap out of her, and she's afraid to get involved with *anyone* right now. Are you willing to tough it out with her?"

"Absolutely." Lynn ignored the barb about her patience, because it was true.

"You haven't tried to force her into anything, have you? I know you can get a little pushy when you want something."

"No," Lynn said vehemently. "I told her *she* would have to be the one to make the first move, because I didn't want her to feel like I was pushing her. We've kissed a few times, but nothing more." Lynn smiled slightly when she recalled dinner at Jessie's house. "She asked me to spend the night with her last week, and I was the one who said no."

"What?" Sarah made a show of placing her hand on Lynn's forehead, and Lynn laughed as she swatted her away. "What's wrong with you? You don't consider that a first move?"

"We'd both been drinking."

"Right, like that's ever stopped you before."

"I'm sick of going home with random women, Sarah." The reality of those words caught Lynn by surprise, but they were, in fact, true. "The night before I drove up here, I went out with my friend Bri. Two different women tried to pick me up, and I went home alone."

"Wow." Sarah looked impressed. "That's definitely not like you, Lynn."

"I'm really tired of living that way, Sarah. I'm sick of waking up in the morning and not remembering the name of the woman in bed next to me."

"Yeah, I can see where being the object of everyone's desire might become tiresome."

"I'm serious." She glanced at her reflection in the wall-length mirror behind the bar. "You used to be the same way. Would you trade what you have with Karen to go back to that?"

"Not in a million years." Sarah grinned. She held her hand up to signal Lynn to wait a minute and picked up the phone. "Family Room."

As Sarah listened to the person on the other end of the line, she glanced at Lynn once, but then walked away, her expression one of obvious concern. Lynn assumed it had something to do with Karen, and she reached in her pocket to get the money to pay for her beer. Sarah came back a moment later, picked up the money, and handed it back to her.

"It's on the house if you'll do something for me."

"What's wrong?"

"That was Jessie. She just got off the phone with Wayne, and he was pretty pissed off about the divorce papers. Can you go check on her?"

"Did she call Karen?" Lynn was already heading for the door.

"Karen had a late dinner meeting in Seattle, and she's spending the night there. I'll get in touch with her, but please call me and let me know that Jessie's all right."

Lynn made it to Jessie's house as fast as she could and jumped out of the car almost before it completely stopped. Jessie pulled the front door open as soon as she knocked.

"Are you all right?" Lynn asked. She rushed in and closed the door behind her, taking the time to make sure that both the handle and the deadbolt were locked. She slid the safety chain into place as well.

"I didn't mean to make everyone so nervous." Jessie went and took a seat in the living room, and Lynn followed close behind her. "I hate it when he calls me like this. I really need to get caller ID for the landline."

Lynn sat next to her but angled her body so she was facing Jessie.

"Listen to me. You need to promise you won't answer the phone again until you do. If anybody needs to get in touch with you, they can call you on your cell." Lynn's heart broke a little when she saw the tears streaking Jessie's face, and she gently rubbed them away. Jessie raised her hand to cover Lynn's and held it against her cheek, relaxing into the touch. "Did he threaten you?"

"No more than usual." Jessie laughed without humor. Lynn hated to break their contact, but she needed to check all the windows and doors to make sure the whole house was locked up tight. When she got to the first window, Jessie spoke again. "I already did that. Everything's taken care of and, besides, he's still in Vegas."

"How do you know that for sure? Because that's what he told you?" Lynn couldn't hide her skepticism. She'd only met Wayne a handful of times and never spent more than five minutes in his presence, but she hated him. Anyone who could put that kind of fear into Jessie deserved nothing less. Lynn continued through the house, then went straight to the kitchen to make a pot of coffee.

"Lynn, you don't have to stay here. I only called Sarah because I was looking for Karen. I just wanted to talk to her."

Lynn didn't respond until she'd returned to the couch. She sat next to Jessie and urged her to lean into her. She tightened her arm around Jessie as she rested her head on Lynn's shoulder and threaded her arms around Lynn's waist.

"I'm not going anywhere, Jess. I told you I'll be here for you whenever you need me, and I intend to follow through. Besides, if I left, I'd never be able to get any sleep because I'd be worrying about you. No matter what arguments we have, or how stupid I behave, I'll always be here."

"I do love you, Lynn. I hope you know that."

"I love you too." Lynn's voice broke, and she wondered how exactly Jessie meant that.

❖

Lynn woke when she heard a phone ringing in the distance. She looked for a clock and finally found one on the DVR under the television. It was nearly one in the morning. She glanced down and saw Jessie was sound asleep right where she'd been earlier, holding tight on to Lynn's waist. The phone stopped ringing, and Lynn closed her eyes again, trying to will herself back to sleep. A few seconds later the phone started ringing again.

Lynn carefully extricated herself from Jessie's grip and began hunting for it, finally realizing the sound was coming from Jessie's purse on the kitchen counter. After a quick glance to see if Jessie was still asleep, she opened it. Her heart tripped when she saw a gun there, right next to Jessie's cell phone. Taking care to not touch the .38—and not really wanting to think about why Jessie would have it in her purse—she grabbed the cell phone and took it out. It had stopped ringing, but started again while she held it. The display told her it was Sarah, so she flipped it open.

"Hello."

"Lynn? Jesus, I was getting ready to close the place and come looking for you two. Is everything okay?"

"Yeah. We fell asleep on the couch." Lynn saw the coffeemaker was still turned on, and she switched it off. She took another look at the gun before closing the purse and pushing it away from her. "I'm sorry I didn't call."

"I'm just glad you're all right. How is she?"

"Scared." Lynn peeked around the corner to check on Jessie, who had leaned over the other way to rest her head on the arm of the couch. "I was afraid to leave her."

"What exactly did he say to her?"

"We honestly didn't talk much, Sarah. I wasn't here for more than a half hour before we fell asleep."

"Well, I called Karen as soon as you left here, and she's on her way back from Seattle, which means she'll probably be there in an hour or so. I'll be there too, as soon as I close up."

"All right. I'll let Jessie know."

"Thank you for being with her, Lynn."

"I'd rather be here than anywhere else, Sarah. You know that."

They hung up, and Lynn decided that maybe she should turn the coffeepot back on. It was probably going to be a long night. She glanced at the purse one last time before heading back out to the living room to wake up Jessie.

CHAPTER FOURTEEN

Jessie opened her eyes when a hand gently shook her shoulder. Looking into Lynn's sky-blue eyes, she smiled and instinctively caressed Lynn's cheek.

"You really are a beautiful woman, Lynn Patrick." She could get lost in the depth of those eyes, and at her words, Lynn's pupils dilated, causing Jessie to suck in a breath. She forced herself to sit up when she felt the stirring of arousal in response to the pure hunger in Lynn's look. "I'm sorry I fell asleep."

"I did too." Lynn swallowed and took a seat next to Jessie. "Your cell phone was ringing. I answered it—I hope that was okay."

"It was in my purse." Jessie looked away when she realized Lynn had to have seen the gun. "Do I smell coffee? In the middle of the night?"

"Jess, what did he say to you?"

"Nothing that he hasn't said a hundred times before." She ran her hands through her hair in an attempt to tame it and let out an exasperated breath before she met Lynn's concerned gaze. "Why don't you ask me what you really want to?"

"I have so many questions I really wouldn't know where to start." Lynn took her hand and their fingers intertwined.

"I bought the gun about two months ago. Rick talked me into it." She absently rubbed her thumb across Lynn's as she spoke. "He's taken me to the shooting range a few times, and I've gotten pretty good, if I do say so myself."

Lynn looked steadily at her, and Jessie fought to not squirm under the scrutiny. She settled back into the couch, and Lynn squeezed her hand gently.

"Do you need the gun? I mean, do you really feel he's an immediate threat?"

"I don't know, Lynn, why don't you tell me? He calls me, and if I don't tell him what he wants to hear, he threatens me. He says he's in Vegas, but as you so wisely pointed out, how do I really know?" She was venting her frustrations on the wrong person, but she couldn't help herself. It was so damned tiring to keep it all bottled up, and what choice did she really have when Amber was around? She had to keep up a strong front for her.

"Come here." Lynn placed an arm around her shoulders, and Jessie began to cry softly when Lynn urged her to rest her head on her chest. Jessie put her arms around her when Lynn kissed the top of her head.

"I'm sorry. This isn't your fault, but I seem to be taking it out on you." Was it foolish to allow herself to feel safe in Lynn's embrace?

"It's okay, baby," Lynn whispered. "I want to help you, but I don't know what to do."

"You're doing it." Jessie sat up and couldn't keep from focusing on Lynn's lips. Before she knew what was happening, her lips were covering Lynn's and she was urging Lynn onto her back. She pulled back for a moment, her breathing erratic. She searched Lynn's eyes for some sign that she wasn't welcome, but she knew she wouldn't see it. Lynn had made it clear that everything was up to her. "I want you, Lynn."

"Jesus, Jess, I want you too, so much." Lynn's voice was barely above a whisper, but she was shaking her head. "But this can't happen right now."

"Why?" Jessie placed tentative fingers on Lynn's hip before moving her hand up and under Lynn's sweater. The muscles of Lynn's abdomen jumped, and Lynn closed her eyes momentarily. "I want this to happen right now."

"Your sister's on her way here. Sarah too, as soon as the bar closes. They're worried about you. Karen's driving back from Seattle."

As if on cue, the doorbell rang, then someone pounded on the front door. Jessie didn't move right away, but stared into Lynn's eyes, making sure Lynn understood what she was about to say.

"This is going to happen, just as soon as we're alone again." She removed her hand from under Lynn's breast and winced at the frustration on Lynn's face. "I feel your pain, believe me. I never knew I could be so aroused, Lynn."

Jessie got to her feet as the pounding on the door started again.

"Jessie! Open the door!" It was Karen, and she sounded frantic.

"I'm coming!" Jessie called. She started toward the door, but Lynn was on her feet and grabbed her by the arm, turning her around to face her. She cupped Jessie's face with both hands and kissed her. Jessie fell into her, offering no resistance to Lynn's tongue as it slipped between her lips. Jessie's knees began to buckle when Lynn pulled away from her.

"There's a little something for you to think about until we're alone again," Lynn said with a grin. She tried to help steady Jessie's legs before letting her go, then began straightening her clothes. Jessie stared at her with what she was sure was a look of pure lust before pulling herself together and going to let her sister in.

"Are you okay?" Karen asked. She closed the door and locked everything again before turning and looking at both of them. "Was he here?"

"No, just on the phone." Jessie noticed a smear of lipstick on the corner of Lynn's mouth and tried to signal her, but Lynn's attention was on Karen. "You didn't have to drive all the way back here from Seattle."

"I was coming back in the morning anyway, and I think I broke land speed records on the way here." Karen took a seat at the dining room table, and Lynn followed. Jessie detoured into the kitchen to get them all cups so they could drink the coffee Lynn had made. When Jessie took her seat, Karen was looking at Lynn with a smirk.

"What?" Lynn asked, obviously self-conscious as her eyes darted back and forth between them before Karen finally took pity on her.

"I can certainly see she was in good hands. That lipstick isn't really your color, is it, Lynn?"

Jessie laughed, and then Lynn's face began to turn red. She stood up and headed for the bathroom.

"So, did I interrupt anything?" Karen asked when she was gone.

"Nothing more than kissing." Jessie crossed her legs and rested her elbows on the table. "You really didn't have to come back tonight."

"Too late, I'm already here." Karen picked up her cup and took a sip. "Are you sure you're all right, Jessie?"

"I had a moment of panic when he called, that's all. I'm sorry I called Sarah and got her all worried about me."

"Hey, don't ever be sorry for calling for help, do you understand me?" Karen grasped Jessie's hand firmly. "I'd be infinitely more upset if you hadn't called and he showed up on your doorstep."

"I know." Jessie forced a smile. God, how she wished she could get on with her life and not have to worry about Wayne every second of the day. Unfortunately, that probably wouldn't happen anytime soon.

"Have you told Mom about this?"

"About what?"

"About you and Lynn." Karen's tone made it clear that Jessie should have known exactly what she was talking about.

"There's nothing to tell." *Not yet, anyway.* She felt her face flush at the thought of Lynn on the couch underneath her and hoped Karen wouldn't notice.

"Not yet." Karen winked as she echoed Jessie's thoughts. "Seriously, Jess, you should tell her. She's completely different since Dad died. You've been a little preoccupied with other matters the past few months and may not have noticed, but trust me on this. It won't be anything like it was when I came out."

Jessie glanced down the hallway at the bathroom door that was still closed. She stared at nothing as she remembered that night eighteen years earlier as though it had happened just yesterday.

Jessie had been fifteen at the time, and Karen was about a month shy of her eighteenth birthday. For reasons Karen had never fully explained, she'd decided to announce to their parents that she was a lesbian.

Arthur Greenfield had been furious. Lynn had planned on spending the night that evening, so the she and Jessie were in the living room watching television. Jessie remembered her father ordering them upstairs to her room so the adults could calmly discuss the situation.

Knowing that no one ever discussed anything "calmly" while her father was around, Jessie had grabbed Lynn's wrist and stopped her halfway up the staircase where they could sit and listen, but still be out of sight. Jessie had felt more than a little betrayed that Karen had kept a secret that big from her. Jessie had always felt they were close enough to talk about anything.

As soon as she and Lynn left the room, her father unleashed the anger he'd kept a tight rein on. Jessie knew her mother was still sitting quietly in the corner, exactly where she'd been when she and Lynn went up the stairs. Where she always was when things took a turn for the worse.

"You are going to a psychiatrist, young lady," he yelled with more vehemence than Jessie had ever heard from him. "First thing in the morning."

"No, I'm not," Karen replied calmly, then laughed out loud.

Jessie had to clasp a hand over her mouth as she turned her head to look at Lynn on the step behind her. Lynn's mouth hung open in disbelief. Karen's response to his statement had scared Jessie almost as much as it excited her. Neither of them had ever dared to challenge their father. He had always been a hateful man, and they'd both learned early in life that they were to do exactly as they were told.

"What did you say to me?"

"There's absolutely nothing wrong with me," Karen stated evenly. "I will not go to a psychiatrist."

"You're sick, Karen," their mother said meekly. "Please listen to your father."

"I certainly will not," Karen replied adamantly. "I am not sick. As a matter of fact, I'm finally happy with who I am. Trying to deny how I feel in order to please the two of you was what made me sick."

"You can't possibly be my daughter," their father said viciously. His voice was lower, but Jessie could still hear the unmistakable anger—the undeniable hatred—in his tone. "No daughter of mine would ever do this to me. You've shamed this family."

"I've shamed this family?" Karen asked angrily. "You're the one who goes out every night and gets drunk off your ass while you're fucking some whore."

Jessie had been so surprised at Karen's choice of language and forceful tone that she almost fell down the stairs. If Lynn hadn't grabbed her arm, she likely would have. The next sound the two of them heard was that of Arthur Greenfield's hand making solid contact with Karen's face. Their mother screamed, but then quickly stifled it on her own, for she and Jessie both knew that if she didn't, her husband would do it for her.

Lynn had to put her arms around Jessie's waist from behind to keep her from running down the stairs to Karen. Jessie struggled against her for a moment, but Lynn's arms held her tight against her body.

"Let go of me!" Karen shouted at her mother, who, Jessie knew from past experience, was trying to help her up.

Jessie settled back into Lynn, who didn't loosen her hold, obviously knowing Jessie would bolt if she did.

"You're just as bad as he is!" Karen yelled. "You know what he does every night, yet you still let him in your bed!"

The three of them fell silent then. Jessie and Lynn sat hidden on the stairs, Lynn one step up, her arms wrapped tight around Jessie.

They were both breathing hard, and Jessie began to think maybe they should get up to her room before they were found out.

"What have you done to Jessica?" her father suddenly roared. "If you've laid a hand on her, so help me I'll kill you!"

"And you think I'm the one who's sick?" Karen asked incredulously.

"Jess?" Lynn asked.

Jessie jumped slightly. She could almost hear her father yelling now, so many years after the fact. A shiver ran down her spine when Lynn's voice jolted her back to the present. She looked at Lynn, who was obviously worried about her. Jessie had been so wrapped up in her memories, she hadn't even been aware Lynn had returned from the bathroom.

"Where were you?"

"Back in my father's house, sitting on the steps with you." Her voice was shaking, but she managed a tremulous smile. If she was completely honest with herself, that had been the night she started developing feelings for Lynn. She loved her for being there for her and for stopping her from doing something foolish.

"The night I came out?" Karen asked. Jessie nodded and looked over at her. Karen shook her head and looked at Lynn. "I thank God every day that you were there when that happened. If you hadn't been there and Jessie had come downstairs to help me, there's no telling how that night would have ended."

After a while, Karen called Sarah to tell her not to bother coming by. When she hung up, she glanced at her watch and groaned. "I'm so happy I don't have to get up in the morning." She smiled at them as she stood up. "Jess, you should come stay with us for a few days. I'd feel better, and I know Sarah would too."

"No, this is my house, and I'm not leaving." She appreciated Karen's concern, but it was time she stopped letting Wayne dictate how she lived her life.

"I'll be here with her," Lynn said.

"I don't want you here if you think I need you to protect me."

"I know you can take care of yourself." Lynn's look convinced Jessie she was telling the truth. "I want to be close, because I know this can't be easy. You might want to talk or something."

Or something is right. Jessie nodded her consent before walking Karen to the door.

"Thank you for being here."

"Don't hesitate to call if you need me," Karen said. Jessie hugged her before ushering her out. "And don't do anything I wouldn't do."

When she shut the door and turned around, Lynn was propped up against the entryway to the kitchen. Jessie walked to her without a word and threaded her arms around Lynn's waist.

"I can't believe how safe you make me feel," she murmured while Lynn held her close. She could feel the rapid beating of Lynn's heart where she rested her head against her shoulder. "If I wasn't so exhausted, I'd try to seduce you."

Lynn laughed and tightened her hold. "I'm pretty beat too. We should get some sleep. I believe you mentioned a spare bedroom the other night?" Lynn pulled back so she could look at Jessie's face.

"You don't have to sleep alone." Jessie caressed Lynn's cheek. Lynn closed her eyes and nestled into the touch.

"I should. We both need the rest, and I'll still be here tomorrow."

Jessie let out a frustrated sigh, which caused Lynn to chuckle, though she stopped abruptly when Jessie stared at her.

"I'm glad you think this is funny, Lynn Patrick. You can sleep in the spare room tonight, but this arrangement won't last long."

She smiled when Lynn's pupils dilated again, her desire transparent. Satisfied with herself, Jessie headed up the stairs to bed.

Chapter Fifteen

Lynn got up before Jessie the next morning and decided to make breakfast. She used the last of the eggs and the bread, and made a mental note to stop at the grocery store later in the day. When the omelets and toast were ready, Jessie still wasn't awake, so Lynn headed upstairs to rouse her.

Her breath caught when she opened the door and saw Jessie lying on the bed, sound asleep, wearing a long T-shirt hiked up to her waist, revealing her bright pink panties. Lynn quietly watched Jessie's serene face. Propping herself against the doorjamb, she continued to stare at her while she thought about how much her perspective on life had changed in the past two weeks.

She'd never made breakfast for anyone—had never wanted to, really—but she wanted to do it for Jessie for the next fifty years. More, if they were lucky enough to live longer. If she was lucky enough to have Jessie's love at all.

It infuriated her that *anyone,* much less Jessie's own husband, could do what Wayne had done. In a perfect world, he'd accept the divorce and walk away, but very little in life was perfect. The chances that he would simply disappear were slim. Jessie would have a hard time moving on with her own life as long as Wayne was still around. Lynn sighed quietly. She'd managed to touch down in the middle of a storm, and the forecast wasn't pleasant. As she silently watched Jessie sleep, she realized this was where she wanted to be, even with the uncertainty surrounding everything.

The telephone shrilled, and she pushed away from the wall. She had taken two steps toward the bed before Jessie groped for the receiver on the nightstand, her eyes still closed.

"Don't." Lynn spoke quickly, just as Jessie was about to grab it. Jessie hesitated and turned to her with sleepy eyes. "It might be Wayne."

Jessie looked at the phone until it stopped ringing. The answering machine picked up, and Lynn held her breath.

"Jessie, I want to apologize for last night." It was Wayne, and Lynn stood still, almost as if she expected him to be able to see her through the phone lines. Jessie sat up quickly and pulled the covers up to her waist. She stared at Lynn, obviously frightened. "Baby, please answer. You know I didn't mean the things I said. You and Amber mean the world to me, and I'd do anything to make you happy."

He sounded so sincere, Lynn might have believed him if she didn't know the truth about him. She finally managed to break her paralysis and went to the bed, where she sat with her back against the headboard. Jessie immediately moved into her arms. She stroked Jessie's hair but felt helpless to stop her soft sobs. In that moment, Lynn understood, to some extent, why women stayed with their abusers. Clearly Jessie wanted to believe what he was saying, if for no other reason than so her daughter would have her father in her life.

"Where the fuck are you at nine o'clock in the morning? Oh, wait, it's December." He laughed, and Jessie gripped Lynn tighter. Lynn knew what was coming and wished she had enough time to get to the machine and turn it off. Instead, she held Jessie and rocked gently back and forth. "Are you with your dyke girlfriend? If I find out you and her...shit, do you see what happens to me? You make me crazy, Jessie. I won't sign these papers. I'll be contesting the divorce, so expect to hear from your lawyer. And you damn well better be keeping all those dykes away from my little girl."

He hung up, and neither of them moved for a few minutes until Jessie pulled away from Lynn. She sat up, wiping the tears from her cheeks.

"Some Prince Charming, huh?" Jessie forced a laugh that turned into a strangled sob when Lynn placed a hand on her back.

"He's a real gem."

"Thank you for not letting me answer it."

"Does his demeanor always change so quickly from sweet to menacing?"

"It's all an act with him. He pretends to be all sweet hoping I'll pick up, but then he goes right into the tirades." Jessie took a deep breath. "How long were you standing there watching me sleep?"

"I'm sorry, I—"

"Don't be sorry. *I'm* sorry that our morning had to start like that." She sniffed at the air and sighed happily. "Do I smell bacon and coffee?"

"I made you breakfast. I was coming up to wake you."

"Give me ten minutes to make myself presentable, and I'll be right down."

❖

"Where's Lynn?" Karen asked when Jessie arrived at her house that evening.

"I invited her, but she said she needed to go back to her parents' house and let her mom know what's going on." Jessie had been disappointed but said, "She'll be back at my place before I get home, so don't worry about it."

"Worry? Why would we worry?" Sarah came out of the kitchen with a wineglass, which she handed to Jessie before giving Karen a quick kiss on the lips. "Just because we love you and really don't want to see any harm come to you?"

"I love you guys too." She sat down then told them about Wayne's phone call that morning.

"And Lynn was there to hear it?" Karen asked.

"All of it." Jessie would have done anything to erase the look of anger on Lynn's face. But then, when Lynn had come to the bed to hold her, she was so happy. She felt truly loved for the first time in her life. "Things were a bit awkward between us afterward."

"How so?" Sarah asked.

"Last night, I made it clear to her that I wanted to sleep with her," Jessie said, surprised that she wasn't embarrassed to admit that. "But after the phone call this morning, I was pretty distant. I think I've been giving her mixed signals."

"Did you sleep with her?" Karen asked.

"No. We were both dead tired, and she stayed in the spare bedroom."

"Jess, she has to realize that he knows exactly what to say in order to push your buttons," Karen told her. "I'm sure she understands why you reacted the way you did."

"Why would she? I'm not sure I understand it myself." Jessie placed her glass on the coffee table and sighed in exasperation. "Why do I continue to let him get to me? He's almost a thousand miles away, and I'm still allowing him to determine how I live my life. I wouldn't be surprised if she gave up on me. I wouldn't blame her."

"That's not going to happen," Sarah said with a chuckle. When Karen and Jessie both looked at her, she shrugged. "I've seen the way she looks at you, Jessie. I was with her for six months, and she never looked at me that way."

A rush of warmth ran through Jessie's body. When Sarah walked into the kitchen to get some appetizers, Karen asked Jessie, "Are you in love with her?"

"I think I am." She nodded, but then thought about Wayne. "Of course, I thought I was in love with Wayne too."

"How do you feel when you're with her?"

"Safe. Loved. Happy. Like I could accomplish anything with her by my side."

"Did Wayne ever make you feel any of those things?"

Jessie thought about it, then looked at Karen and simply shook her head.

"Jessie, if Wayne is the only reason you haven't slept with Lynn, you need to reassess the situation. I'm not trying to talk you into doing something you don't want to. But if you do, you need to consider why you haven't. The night you and Lynn had a fight, and the days after, you were more upset than I've ever seen you. No matter what you ultimately decide, just know that Sarah and I are here for you."

"Oh, my God, I just had a brilliant idea!" Sarah exclaimed as she walked back into the living room. She waited until she had their attention before springing it on them. She pointed at Jessie. "You're going to win Lynn in the auction tomorrow night."

Jessie laughed. "I don't have that kind of money."

"I'll help with the money. It's for a good cause, and you'll end up with the girl. It's brilliant, admit it." Jessie and Karen both laughed at Sarah's self-satisfied smirk.

"You're brilliant, honey."

"I really don't want to take your money. How much do you think she'll go for?" Jessie was already calculating how much she'd be able to spend on her own. The more she thought about it, the better the idea sounded.

"I've been to a few of these before, and the most I've ever seen someone bring was about a thousand. But that was in Frisco. I've never seen anybody go for anywhere near that here." Sarah sat down next to Karen and kissed her cheek. "How much do you love me right now?"

"I'll withhold my answer to that until *after* you tell us who went for that much, and who bought her."

"That's how I met Lynn, but what's the big deal?"

"You spent a thousand dollars for a date with Lynn Patrick?" Karen asked.

"That's only a drop in the bucket compared to what I'd be willing to spend to go out with you, sweetie." Sarah tilted her head and batted her eyes, causing Jessie and Karen to laugh.

"Nice answer," Jessie said between fits of giggling. If the bidding got any higher than five hundred dollars, she wouldn't be able to win on her own, but she was sure going to try. She didn't want to take money from Sarah, but she wasn't above it. "I told her this morning I wasn't going to the auction. Maybe I'll surprise her by showing up after all."

Chapter Sixteen

When Jessie walked into the bar around six Friday night, a huge crowd of women was already present. She strode to Sarah's office, briefly knocked, then handed Sarah a piece of paper.

Lynn had been asleep by the time Jessie arrived home from Karen's the night before, and while she seriously considered crawling into the spare bed with her, she decided she could wait another day or two. Of course if she didn't win the auction, she might end up waiting longer than that.

"This is the most you can spend?" Sarah asked after looking it over.

"I might be able to go another fifty, but then you and Karen would have to forgo your Christmas present this year." Jessie smiled innocently, knowing exactly what Sarah's response would be.

"I don't think Karen would ever forgive me if I made that deal." She opened the top drawer of her desk and pulled out an envelope containing a small stack of twenties. "I can give you another two hundred, which gives you an even seven hundred to work with. Are you sure you want to do it this way? You don't want her to know you're bidding?"

"I want it to be a surprise."

"What if you don't win?"

"I'd be very pissed, because I sure don't want to be sitting at home while she's out on a date doing God knows what with some other woman."

"And what exactly will *you* do with her if you win?"

"The date is for dinner, right? Whatever happens after that—" Jessie shrugged. Over her shoulder, she said, "God only knows."

Sarah's laughter rang as she pulled the door shut behind her. She hadn't gone more than two steps before she ran right into Lynn. Jessie took a step back and let her gaze travel slowly over Lynn's body. She looked outstanding in a tuxedo, but all Jessie could think about was getting her out of it. Her face warmed as she forced herself to meet Lynn's eyes.

"Wow."

"I could say the same about you." Lynn grinned and took in Jessie's curves, causing Jessie's face to flame. Lynn gently took hold of her arm and led her out of the path of customers. "I thought you said you weren't coming tonight."

"I changed my mind. I decided I didn't want to miss it."

"Great, like I'm not nervous enough without you here to witness this." Lynn took a deep breath and looked around at the people crowding the bar, raking her fingers quickly through her hair. The resulting mess was the sexiest thing Jessie had ever seen.

"Why would I make you nervous?"

"I didn't want to do this, Jess. You talked me into it."

"Okay, what does that have to do with anything?"

Lynn shifted her weight and glanced around quickly. She shook her head when she turned back to Jessie.

"I've been involved with these things before. Some women think if they spend money to go out with you, they deserve to get something more than dinner in return."

"So you're telling me you're going to have sex with whoever wins you in the auction tonight?"

Jessie let her concern show when Lynn looked as if she might faint. She took Lynn's hand and gave it a gentle squeeze.

"Are you all right?"

"I'm fine," Lynn said after a moment.

"Answer the question."

"No, that's not what I was saying. I said *some* women, not *all* women. But even if the woman who wins me is one of them, I do know how to say no." Lynn moved closer, and Jessie breathed faster. She stroked Lynn's cheek.

"Maybe I need to make something clear, Jess. I want *you*. I want to make love to *you*. I don't even want to go on a date with anyone else, because it'll take away from the time I could be spending with you. Even if I can't ever have you."

Jessie was afraid her knees might give out, and she put her arms around Lynn's neck, pulling her closer. Lynn pressed her against the wall as their lips met in a hungry kiss. Jessie moaned into her mouth when Lynn shifted her hips against her, but then an arm between them pushed Lynn away. Jessie shivered at the loss of contact and glared at Karen, who was trying her best to look stern.

"No testing the merchandise. If we let you, then we have to let everyone." Karen looked back and forth between them as she spoke. "Besides, if these women think you two are together, we'll be lucky to get fifty dollars for Lynn, and that would likely come out of my own pocket. Understand?"

Jessie nodded, but she never took her eyes off Lynn. Lynn shot a dirty look in Karen's direction before turning a much softer expression Jessie's way.

"I'll see you later."

When she was gone, Jessie rounded on Karen. "You better hope to God she doesn't go for more than seven hundred. If someone else wins this thing, I'll never speak to you again."

"Hey, this was Sarah's idea!"

"And since Sarah's your partner, I'll never speak to either one of you again." Jessie took a deep breath before she turned and walked away.

❖

Lynn stood on the stage trying to calm her breathing, but not having much success. Why the hell did she ever agree to this? She tried desperately to find Jessie in the sea of darkness that engulfed all but the first couple rows of women but couldn't see anything. She glanced over at Sarah, who stood a few feet away from her, running the auction.

"All right, ladies, we have a famous author here who grew up in this area, but is now living in San Francisco. She's only in town for a few days, so the date with her will have to take place in the next week." Sarah had a piece of paper in her hand that she hadn't been holding when she was auctioning the other women off. Lynn rubbed her sweaty palms on her trousers and tried to look like she was having the time of her life. "I have instructions here from an anonymous bidder, so you won't only be bidding against one another. We're going to start at fifty dollars. Do I hear fifty?"

"Fifty!"

Lynn tuned everything out when Sarah told the crowd that the anonymous bidder was going to seventy-five, at which point the bids came in so fast Lynn couldn't keep up. What seemed to her like hours must have been only a few minutes, and Karen brought her attention back when she spoke briefly in Sarah's ear.

"Okay ladies, our anonymous bidder has just upped the ante. Our last bid was seven hundred and fifty dollars. Our anonymous bidder has gone to eight hundred. Do I hear eight fifty?"

Lynn looked down at her feet, wondering who the anonymous person was. She hoped it was Jessie, but she didn't have that kind of money, especially with a young daughter and no husband. She ran her hand through her hair and willed the damn thing to end soon. She just wanted to get off the stage and disappear.

"Eight hundred, going once, going twice," Sarah paused. "Sold, for eight hundred dollars."

That was all Lynn needed to hear. She turned quickly and left the stage, practically running to Sarah's office, where she knew Karen would be waiting.

"All right, tell me who the hell this anonymous bidder was," she said before she closed the door behind her.

"I don't know." Karen sat back in the chair and refused to look away. "I just know she wanted to remain anonymous."

"So how are we going to set up this date?"

"We already have. You're supposed to meet her here at seven o'clock tomorrow night." Karen slid a piece of paper across the desk and shrugged when Lynn raised an eyebrow.

Though Lynn had been hoping it would be Jessie, she didn't recognize the handwriting. "I am *never* doing this again." She took a seat and dropped her head back. The door opened and Jessie walked in with Lynn's parents, Charlie, and a woman Lynn had never met before. Charlie introduced her as his new girlfriend.

"Congrats, big sister. You went for way more than any of those other women." Charlie gave her a playful punch in the arm as she stood to face them. "I had no idea my sister was so popular with the ladies."

"Who won you?" Jessie asked.

"I was hoping it was you."

"I was the anonymous bidder, but I only authorized Sarah to go as high as seven hundred. I have no idea who jumped in after that."

"Sarah never indicated it was someone new." Lynn looked at Karen.

"I figured it was easier to let Sarah think it was the same bidder, rather than try to explain we had another woman who wanted to stay behind the scenes." Karen looked at everyone in the office, then returned her attention to Lynn. "It wasn't like I had a lot of time to explain to her what was going on. I only said the anonymous bidder put in a higher bid."

"But you know who it is." Jessie took a step toward Karen. "You'll tell me, right?"

"I can't reveal that information. That's the whole point of being anonymous." Karen crossed her arms over her chest and glared at them all, almost as though daring them to push her. Her eyes settled on Lynn last. "Lynn will find out who it is tomorrow night at seven."

"I'm going home." Lynn turned to Jessie. "Did you drive here?"

"Yes. I told Sarah I'd help her out here for a while though. I don't know when I'll be there. You have a key, right?"

"Yeah. I'll see you later." She pushed her way past everyone, refusing to look anyone in the eye. As soon as the date was over the following evening, she'd concentrate on making things move forward between her and Jessie.

CHAPTER SEVENTEEN

Lynn stood before Jessie for one final inspection before she headed to the bar to meet her date. It was all so ridiculous. She had no desire to be going out on a date, especially when Jessie would be sitting at home by herself. Lynn didn't care what she looked like because she wasn't trying to impress anyone. She struggled to keep her hands to herself when Jessie tried to straighten her collar.

"You really need to hold still."

"I'm sorry." Lynn took a deep breath, but when Jessie's fingers brushed her collarbone, she took both of Jessie's hands. "Why can't I cancel this and just stay here with you? We could order a pizza and rent a movie or something."

"That's tempting, but you have an obligation to fulfill." Jessie shook her head and pulled her hands out of Lynn's grasp as she took a step back. "And based on the way you're looking at me right now, I'm pretty sure pizza and a movie isn't the only thing on your mind."

"You've got that right."

Jessie placed one hand firmly on Lynn's chest, right above her breasts. Her eyes focused on Lynn's lips, and Lynn closed her eyes momentarily against the rush of arousal. She could see the desire that mirrored her own and couldn't stop her swift intake of breath. Jessie smiled, obviously satisfied with her reaction.

When Lynn tried to kiss her, Jessie pulled away with a wisp of a smile. "You have a date to go on, stud."

"Jess," Lynn said, hating that she sounded like a whiny kid. She sat down on the couch and, elbows on her knees, she held her head in her hands. She was shaking so much she wasn't sure she could stand on her own again. This was torture, plain and simple. She finally looked up when Jessie didn't respond. She was standing a few feet away, watching her. "Doesn't this bother you?"

"Of course it does, but I'm the one who encouraged you to do it in the first place, so I have only myself to blame." She placed a hand under Lynn's chin and turned her head, forcing Lynn to look at her. "But if you sleep with this woman tonight, I'll never forgive you."

"I swear to you, nothing will happen. I'll meet her and have a drink or two, then tell her I'm not feeling well. I can be back here by eight."

Lynn was sure her disappointment was obvious when Jessie laughed and placed a chaste kiss on her cheek.

"I'll be here when you get back, Lynn. Don't cut the date short because of me. If you do that, she might expect you to go out with her again."

"Shit, I didn't think of that." Lynn shoved a hand through her hair and sighed. "All right, but I *will* be back early. When dinner's over, that's it."

Deciding then that she wanted to hurry up and go so she could get the whole thing over with, she stood, pulled Jessie to her feet and kissed her quickly, then grabbed her keys and walked out the door. The entire evening was going to be pure hell.

❖

"That was your mystery date," Sarah said as she hung up the phone and faced Lynn. "She's running a little late, but she'll be here before eight."

"Do you have any idea how close I am to canceling this and leaving?" Lynn looked at her watch for the millionth time since taking a seat at the end of the bar to wait. It was almost seven thirty, for God's sake. She could have been sitting on the couch wearing sweatpants with Jessie by her side instead of waiting for a woman she didn't even want to see so she could take her out to a dinner she didn't want. "Do you know who she is?"

"Nope, Karen wouldn't tell me." Sarah shrugged in a way that indicated she knew damn well who it was, but didn't intend to tell Lynn.

Lynn rested her head in her hands. "You people are trying to kill me, aren't you?"

"What was that, sweetie? It's kind of loud in here tonight."

"Nothing. Give me another drink. Maybe the evening will go by quicker if I'm drunk."

❖

Jessie walked into the bar at ten minutes to eight and immediately spotted Lynn, sitting with her back to the doors. Jessie grinned, knowing Lynn had chosen to sit that way on purpose so she wouldn't have to see her date walk in.

"Is this seat taken?"

Lynn turned to look at her, and Jessie somehow managed not to laugh at the surprise on Lynn's face. Her body heated noticeably when Lynn's eyes moved slowly down the length of her in order to take her all in. Jessie was glad she'd decided to wear the slinky black dress. She'd have to wear it more often if it meant Lynn would look at her that way.

"What are you doing here?"

"I'm your date for the evening."

"But I thought...I mean, you said..."

"You're cute when you're flustered," Jessie said as she took a seat. "Has anyone ever told you that?"

"I've never been flustered. These past couple of weeks I've felt a lot of things I never have."

"Something to drink?" Sarah asked.

"How did this happen, and why didn't you tell me?" Lynn asked, completely ignoring Sarah.

"I wanted it to be a surprise. And as far as how it happened— maybe you should talk to your parents about that." Jessie couldn't take her eyes off Lynn. She wanted to skip dinner and go straight home so they could do what they should have done a long time ago. Jessie wasn't sure she could wait much longer. Being in Lynn's presence seemed to put her in a constant state of arousal.

"My parents? My father actually had something to do with this? He paid so you could win me at an auction?"

"Okay, I'll check back with you two later." Sarah walked away, whistling.

"He cares about you, Lynn. They knew how badly I wanted this, and they helped me out. After the auction, when you asked me, I honestly didn't know." Jessie placed a hand over Lynn's, which was resting on the bar. "I cried when they told me. It was the nicest thing anyone's ever done for me."

"Well, it seems they love you *almost* as much as I do." Lynn stared into Jessie's eyes for a moment, and Jessie had to look away when it became too intense because she was certain she would dissolve into a puddle. "I know we're both dressed up and ready to party, but can we go back to your place and have that pizza and watch a movie? I really don't feel like going out right now."

"I thought you'd never ask."

CHAPTER EIGHTEEN

A re you really interested in this movie?" Jessie's head had been in Lynn's lap, but she sat up and ran a finger along Lynn's jaw as she spoke. She grinned when Lynn closed her eyes and shuddered.

"I'm not even sure I know what's happening."

"In the movie?" Jessie raised one eyebrow when Lynn opened her eyes.

"Yes, in the movie, you smartass." Lynn leaned forward to kiss Jessie. "I'm fully aware of what's happening between us."

Jessie shifted slightly so she was facing Lynn, took her hands, and pulled Lynn on top of her. Jessie closed her eyes and lifted her hips as she let out a contented sigh.

When Lynn's mouth covered hers, Jessie parted her lips to allow Lynn's tongue room to explore. Her hands on Lynn's butt, she urged her closer, grinding her pelvis into her. Lynn pulled back slightly and rested her forehead against Jessie's.

"Are you sure about this?" Lynn asked when Jessie opened her eyes.

"Lynn, I really like where this is going." Jessie brought her hands up the curve of Lynn's ass and continued up her back. "Please, don't stop."

The way her jeans were pressing against her was driving Jessie crazy. She wanted to be naked in Lynn's arms, and she wanted—needed—it to be soon.

"If I do something you don't like, I want you to tell me, all right?"

"I need you to touch me, Lynn." Jessie knew she sounded desperate, but she didn't care. She needed to feel Lynn's body, and she didn't want to wait any longer. "Let's go upstairs."

Lynn got to her feet without a word and held a hand out to Jessie to help her up. Jessie stepped into her arms and pressed her lips to the hollow of Lynn's throat, causing Lynn's head to fall back and eliciting a groan.

"My knees may give out if we don't get upstairs soon," Lynn murmured. She took hold of Jessie's hand and led her to the master bedroom.

Lynn stopped right inside the door and Jessie pulled her into an embrace, grasping the bottom of the sweatshirt Lynn had put on when they'd returned from the bar. Lynn tried to unbutton Jessie's shirt, but her hands were shaking, and she couldn't seem to get the buttons through the holes. Jessie stilled her hands and brought them to her lips.

"Rip it off. I need to feel you against me now, Lynn." Jessie had never been the aggressor when it came to sex, but she wanted Lynn so badly she couldn't control her desires. She watched in wonder as Lynn's pupils dilated, and when Lynn ripped open her shirt, she walked Lynn backward to the bed, pushing her down onto the mattress when the backs of her knees touched it.

"You are so beautiful." Jessie stared at Lynn and let her shirt fall to the floor, then reached behind her back to undo her bra. Lynn quickly removed her own bra and tossed it on the floor as Jessie hastily shed her pants and underwear. Lynn was propped up on her elbows, her feet on the floor, when Jessie straddled her, leaving the evidence of her desire on Lynn's sweatpants. Lynn sat up and placed a hand firmly in the middle of Jessie's back, urging her closer so she could take a nipple into her mouth. Jessie put her arms around Lynn's neck, holding Lynn's head tight against her breast as her own head fell back. "God, yes."

Jessie was so aroused she was almost in pain. She forced her hips to stop moving because she was certain she would come any second. That wasn't how she wanted her first time with a woman—with Lynn—to be. She pulled away and looked into Lynn's eyes, both of them breathing heavily.

"Take your pants off." She rolled off Lynn and onto her side. Lynn made quick work of the clothes she still had on, and then she was lying next to Jessie, their naked bodies pressed tight together. "You feel so damn good."

Jessie ran her hand down Lynn's abdomen, but she stopped, suddenly nervous, when the muscles tightened under her fingers and Lynn moaned. Jessie pulled her hand away.

"Jess, what's wrong?"

"I'm afraid I might disappoint you." Jessie looked away. Where had the lump in her throat come from? She closed her eyes and took a deep breath. This was definitely the worst possible time to develop performance anxiety.

"Ah, God, you could never disappoint me, Jess." She touched Jessie's cheek, gently turning her head back so she could look into her eyes. "I love you, Jessie, and that's all that matters."

"I've never done this before," Jessie said, as if Lynn wasn't already aware of her inexperience. She had to force herself to not look away again. "What if I can't...satisfy you?"

"Then we'll have a lot of fun practicing until you get it right. You may not believe it, but that isn't what this is about for me. This is about sharing something intimate with you. You can't even begin to imagine how I feel about you—how I've always felt about you, for as long as I can remember."

"How do you always seem to know exactly the right things to say?" Jessie asked. Lynn smiled and shrugged. Jessie tried to kiss her, but Lynn pulled back, obviously not finished.

"I'm not worried about what happens—or even what doesn't happen—in this bed here tonight."

Lynn threaded her fingers through Jessie's hair and pulled her close before kissing her passionately. Lynn pushed Jessie onto her back and propped herself up on one elbow so she could look at her face.

"Physical satisfaction, if it doesn't happen tonight," Lynn said quietly, her fingertips skimming across Jessie's midsection, "will certainly come in time. I have absolutely no doubt."

Jessie closed her eyes and enjoyed the way Lynn was touching her. She wasn't entirely convinced Lynn meant what she was saying or if she was only trying to help her relax. Either way, her words were having a rather profound effect.

"What if we spend the next twenty years together and I still haven't managed to get the hang of this?" Jessie waited for Lynn to look at her and tried not to melt under Lynn's smoldering look. A gasp escaped her as Lynn's wandering fingers moved down below her belly button. Her heart stuttered as the words she'd spoken took hold. It was presumptuous of her to think Lynn would be viewing this in terms of years, not days. She held her breath while she waited for Lynn to respond.

Lynn was silent as she appeared to consider the question, and her eyes moved down to where her fingers stopped their exploration. She shook her head after a moment and removed her hand before looking at Jessie's face again.

"No," she finally said. Jessie would have taken her seriously if not for the grin Lynn was obviously trying to hide. "I think if it took any more than ten years, I'd probably have to kick you to the curb."

"Then I guess I'd better keep practicing until I get it right." Jessie relaxed slightly with their banter, pure arousal quickly replacing her tension. "If that's okay with you."

"That is definitely okay with me, as long as I'm the one you'll be practicing with." Jessie turned onto her side to face Lynn, whose hand moved slowly from Jessie's shoulder down toward her hip.

"I don't want to practice with anyone but you." Jessie marveled at the way her skin tingled under Lynn's touch. She wanted Lynn more than she'd ever thought it possible to want anyone. Lynn's hand moved lightly across Jessie's hip as their lips touched, and she was gone. She lost herself in the passion and allowed her instincts to take over. She moaned softly when Lynn's tongue caressed her bottom lip, and Lynn groaned in pleasure when Jessie rolled onto her back, pulling Lynn over on top of her.

Jessie slowly felt her way up Lynn's torso and Lynn kissed her neck before moving down to her shoulders. Jessie let her head drop back and closed her eyes. Her entire body hummed as Lynn's tongue gently caressed a nipple.

Lynn's hand moved down Jessie's leg, then slowly back up the inside of her thigh, leaving a trail of fire in its wake. Jessie let her legs fall open and moaned in pleasure when Lynn's fingers found the swollen, aching flesh between her legs. "Ah, Jessie," Lynn murmured when she encountered the liquid heat. Jessie moaned in pleasure and her hips lifted slightly. Lynn's fingers slid easily through the wet folds and entered her slowly. Lynn moved back up to look into Jessie's eyes. "You're so incredibly wet for me."

"Yes," Jessie said on a breath. She struggled to keep her eyes open. "It's all for you, Lynn. All I have to do is think about you."

"This is your last chance to change your mind." Jessie simply stared at her in disbelief. "Once I start, I won't want to stop."

The anxiety Jessie had felt before had completely dissipated, and she had never been more relaxed or in control of what she was doing. It seemed to be the most natural thing in the world. It was right. In her heart, she knew that.

"I have to be completely honest with you here, honey," Jessie said, her hips continuing to roll insistently against Lynn's hand. She finally allowed her eyes to close, arching her neck in the process. "If you don't finish what you've started, I might be forced to seriously hurt you."

Lynn laughed—a deep rich sound that sent a jolt of electricity through Jessie—before she ran her tongue down Jessie's exposed neck. Jessie raised her arms above her head and held the pillow tight when Lynn began to thrust, her fingers buried inside her.

"God, Jess, you're incredibly gorgeous," Lynn whispered into her ear before leaving a trail of wet kisses down her neck and torso. She paused once in her journey to glance up at Jessie, her fingers never relenting. "I need to taste you, Jess. Can I please taste you?"

"Yes," Jessie hissed, her body crying out for release. She tensed momentarily when she felt Lynn's hot breath on her clitoris. She arched her back slightly and a rush of excitement surged through her as Lynn's tongue began to explore the fire between her legs. She was aware of absolutely nothing other than the ecstasy she felt as Lynn's mouth closed around her clit, sucking on it gently.

"You feel so fucking amazing," Jessie managed to murmur while she met Lynn's insistent thrusts. She groaned when Lynn's free hand moved to her breast, squeezing an erect nipple between her thumb and forefinger. Jessie's body tensed at the first signs of orgasm, and she reached down to hold Lynn's mouth tight against her.

Within moments—while Lynn's tongue worked her clit unrelentingly—Jessie cried out in undeniable pleasure. Her body shuddered uncontrollably with the intensity of her climax, and Lynn continued to stroke her. Just when Jessie started to think the exquisite feeling was ending, Lynn sent her sailing again. Jessie's heart was pounding so hard by the time the second orgasm subsided, she was sure it would beat right out of her chest.

Lynn crawled up to lie beside her, both of them breathing as if they'd just finished running a marathon. They held each other tight, and Jessie's body continued to shudder with aftershocks. Jessie groaned with the pleasure of the weight of Lynn's thigh pressed firmly against her throbbing center. Tears of contentment, of relief, of joy and pleasure spilled down her cheeks.

"What's wrong?" Lynn pulled away from Jessie and brushed the hair from her eyes. The concern was not only evident in her voice, but in her expression. Jessie shook her head and cupped Lynn's jaw.

"Nothing. I'm great." She kissed Lynn gently, then added with a contented sigh, "*You're* great."

"Why, thank you, darlin'," Lynn replied with a sigh that conveyed her contentment. "Turn on your other side. I want to hold you for a while."

"What about you?" Jessie wanted to bring Lynn to the heights she'd just experienced, but she couldn't deny she was nervous. Lynn kissed her, then shifted both of them so Jessie's backside was cradled against her.

"I'm fine, and I'm not going anywhere." Lynn's mouth was

close to her ear, and Jessie shivered. "There'll be plenty of time for you to practice."

Neither of them said another word, and Jessie felt more content than ever before. She closed her eyes and drifted off, experiencing the most peaceful night's sleep she'd had in months.

CHAPTER NINETEEN

L ynn woke the next morning when her phone rang. After she managed to pull herself away from the warm body next to her and reach down for her sweatpants, she sighed. It was her mother.

"Hi, Mom." She turned onto her back with a grin. Jessie faced her and laid her head on Lynn's shoulder, wrapping an arm snugly around her waist.

"So how was your date last night?" The happiness in her mother's voice was evident, and Lynn chuckled.

"You got me." Lynn looked down at Jessie, who was about to take a nipple into her mouth, threaded her fingers through Jessie's hair, and pulled her away from her destination. Jessie laughed quietly, raising her head. "Thank you for what you did."

"No problem, honey. The two of you were meant to be together, and we finally decided we needed to give you a push in the right direction. Believe it or not, it was your father's idea. I didn't interrupt anything, did I?"

"Of course not." Lynn tried not to react to Jessie's hand, which was slowly moving up the inside of her thigh. Because she hadn't come the night before, the morning's contact was akin to cruelty. "I have to go, though. I'll call you later, okay?"

Lynn closed the phone and tossed it on the floor without waiting for her mother's response. She pushed Jessie onto her back and looked down at her.

"You are evil, Jessica Greenfield. I was trying to have a

conversation with my mother. The woman who made last night possible. Remember her?"

"You'll have to remind me to thank her the next time I see her." Jessie's hands were still roaming Lynn's body, causing a fire that Lynn was having trouble dealing with.

"Good morning."

"It is a wonderful morning." Jessie tried to push Lynn off her, but Lynn refused to budge. "I want you on your back. Now."

"I never pictured you as a top." Lynn bent to kiss the underside of Jessie's chin. When she was preoccupied with that, Jessie forced Lynn onto her back. Lynn smiled up at her. "Very nice moves you've got there."

Lynn let out a rush of air when Jessie positioned herself so her leg was between Lynn's and pressing firmly against Lynn's center. She put her arms around Jessie and pulled her close, unable to stop her pelvis from rocking against her.

"I want you so much, Jess," she whispered into her ear, gasping for breath. The night before, she'd worried that Jessie hadn't wanted to reciprocate. She was still concerned about that, and despite her growing need for release, she said, "You don't have to do this, baby."

"I know I don't, but I want to. I want you to come for me, Lynn. Will you do that?"

"Yes." Lynn let her head fall back and she closed her eyes as Jessie's tongue danced around a nipple. Jessie's hand continued its journey across Lynn's abdomen, then downward as Lynn opened her legs to allow Jessie more room to explore. She groaned at the loss of the intense pressure when Jessie's thigh shifted away from her.

"Tell me what you need," Jessie whispered, her fingers between Lynn's legs. Lynn opened her eyes and looked at her, the uncertainty obvious in Jessie's tremulous tone. "Help me love you, Lynn."

Lynn met Jessie's eyes as she took Jessie's wrist, pushing it slowly toward the place she needed her, then guiding her fingers inside. She fought the urge to close her eyes again and held Jessie's gaze as Jessie took her, claiming her in a way that no other woman ever had. Lynn gave herself freely and offered her heart in the process. Jessie took it with no hesitation, and Lynn finally closed her eyes when Jessie touched her lips to Lynn's abdomen, right above the triangle of hair between her legs.

"Do you want my mouth on you?"

"Ah, God…please…yes." Lynn whimpered. She'd never wanted anyone as much as she wanted Jessie. And she'd never again *need* anyone the way she needed her right now. No one had ever been able to make her feel so alive.

Lynn almost burst when Jessie's warm breath brushed over her swollen sex. She groaned and moved her hips gently against Jessie's hand and tongue. Within moments, Lynn's muscles tightened around Jessie's fingers, and she let out a long, low-pitched moan as the orgasm overtook her. Jessie didn't stop until Lynn grabbed her wrist and pulled her away, then held her close as they kissed with even more passion than the night before.

"I don't think you'll have to practice much," Lynn said, her voice raspy and the aftermath of her incredible orgasm still humming through her nerve endings. She exhaled slowly as she looked at Jessie. "If I didn't know better, I'd think you've done this before."

"Well, I've seen a few movies. And I've read a few books. You can learn a lot from books."

"Apparently so." Lynn chuckled as she pushed Jessie's hair out of her eyes.

"There's this one book in particular that I really liked," Jessie said, placing a hand on Lynn's abdomen. "Lynn Patrick wrote it. Ever heard of her?"

"I might have." Lynn grinned as she put a hand on top of Jessie's. "What did you like about it?"

"I have a sneaking suspicion it was about me. Was it?"

"Yes. I didn't think you'd ever read it." Lynn couldn't hide her embarrassment, but Jessie lifted Lynn's hand and kissed it.

"So…I did all right?" Jessie asked.

"Baby, you were incredible. Amazing. Astounding. Mind-blowing." Jessie laughed and moved so she was lying next to Lynn. She settled in with her head on Lynn's shoulder and her arm draped possessively across her torso. "Are you okay with this?"

"No regrets, Lynn," Jessie replied. Lynn took Jessie's hand and held it tight against her chest. "It was everything I thought it would be. *You* were everything I thought you would be. You're a very attentive lover. My emotions are a bit all over the place right now, but yeah. I'm okay with it."

Lynn closed her eyes, unable to stop the goofy grin she knew was on her face.

They stayed like that for a few minutes, until Jessie suddenly pulled away. Lynn had been close to dozing off again, but the immediate loss of contact startled her back into consciousness.

"I need food. I feel like I haven't eaten in weeks." Jessie put on a robe and disappeared into the bathroom.

When Jessie shut the door behind her, Lynn got out of bed and put on the sweats she'd been wearing the night before. She glanced back at the unkempt bed and smiled. For the first time in her life, she was truly happy. Life was good.

❖

"Amber will be home tomorrow, right?" Lynn asked while they were doing the dishes after a fantastic breakfast of French toast and bacon.

"Tomorrow night, yes. Their plane gets in at six."

"Do you need me to go back to my parents' house?" Lynn had been dreading the answer all morning. It might be uncomfortable for Jessie with Amber there, and Lynn wasn't used to having to censor her speech or her actions. Jessie turned the water off and faced Lynn, then rested against the counter, her head tilted to the side.

"Why would I want you to leave?"

"It might be easier for you if I wasn't here." Lynn continued drying the dishes but stopped when Jessie took the towel away from her. She took Lynn's arms and wrapped them around her before kissing her on the cheek.

"I want you here, Lynn. I'm going to have to tell Amber that things are going to be different from now on. I don't know if she's old enough to understand all of it, but I don't want to keep anything from her. I'll tell her as much as she can handle. How do you think she'll deal with having a lesbian mom?"

"*Are* you a lesbian?" Lynn pulled back enough to meet Jessie's eyes and held her breath while she waited for the answer. Jessie's response would determine her own future, one way or the other.

"You have to ask that after last night and this morning?" Jessie stroked Lynn's cheek with the back of her fingers.

"I'm serious, Jess." Lynn led her to the couch and they sat next to each other. "What happened between us doesn't make you a lesbian. It doesn't make you anything other than curious. It's what's in your head, and your heart, that makes you a lesbian."

"You know me well enough to realize I'd never do what we did simply out of curiosity." Jessie looked down at their hands as their fingers entwined. "I was more nervous than I'd ever been about having sex with another woman, but I've never felt desire for anyone like I feel for you. I wouldn't have slept with you if I wasn't sure that I was a lesbian."

"And you want to tell Amber about it so soon?"

"She's six going on twenty," Jessie said with a laugh. Lynn relaxed slightly at the sound. "I'm hoping you'll be spending a lot of time here, and I need to tell her something. I don't want to lie to her. Will you stay and help me tell her?"

"Yes." Lynn pulled her closer and buried her face in Jessie's hair, breathing in her scent. "I've never wanted anything more."

"Then stop worrying. I'll pick them up, drop off my mother at home, and be back here so the three of us can have dinner together."

"Not quite ready to tell your mother?"

"Not quite. I'll see how the ride home with her goes. I don't want to wait too long, because I don't want to hide this. I want the whole world to know."

"Me too." She quickly kissed Jessie, then had an idea. "Come with me to my mother's Christmas Eve party."

"I usually spend Christmas Eve with Karen and Sarah."

"Bring them too. I want you to be there." Lynn pulled away from Jessie and took her cell phone from her pocket. "All of my extended family will be there, and I want them to meet Amber. I'm sure at some point over the years *you've* already met most of them."

"Are you sure it'd be all right?"

Lynn held up the phone before opening it and pressing the speed-dial number for her mother. She waited impatiently for her to answer, returning to the kitchen and pacing back and forth in front of the sink.

"Mom, would it be okay if I brought someone to your Christmas Eve party?"

"Someone? Is it someone I know? And is that how you greet your mother?"

"Hi, Mom. Actually, it's Jessie and Amber. And probably Karen and Sarah too."

"That's four someones. I don't know if I have room for four more."

"It's a party, for God's sake." Lynn knew her mother was pulling her strings, because she could still hear the joy in her voice. "It's not like you need to fit them in at the table for dinner."

"Of course it's all right, Lynn. I fully expected you to bring Jessie and Amber, and what's a couple more? Your grandmother would love to meet Amber, and I'm sure Charlie's children would love to play with her."

"Thanks, Mom. You're the best." Lynn hung up and hugged Jessie to her. "My mother loves you. My whole family loves you."

"And I love your whole family." Jessie snuggled back in Lynn's arms. "I just hope my mother doesn't have a problem with this."

"Even if she does, I'll still be here for you, Jess." Lynn kissed her on the lips and hugged her tight. "I'll always be here for you."

"So you've told me. I really like the way that sounds." Jessie pulled away from her and went back to finish the dishes. "Do you have any plans for the rest of the day?"

"Spending it in bed with you." Lynn bumped her with her hip, and Jessie laughed.

"I'll make you a deal. I promised Amber I'd have a Christmas tree up and decorated by the time she got back from Florida. You help me with that, then we can go to bed early tonight."

"Early? Like three o'clock, maybe?" Lynn couldn't hide how happy she was and had no desire to. Jessie made her feel like a kid again, and she didn't intend to let that feeling go.

"You're so bad." Jessie laughed and smacked her with the dishtowel. "I was thinking more like two o'clock."

CHAPTER TWENTY

Jessie got Amber buckled into her car seat and her mother situated on the passenger side before stowing their luggage in the trunk. Jessie had met them in baggage claim, and since then, Amber had talked nonstop about how much fun she'd had meeting Mickey Mouse. Apparently, she'd forgotten all about the telephone incident.

"So, dear, what have you been doing while we were gone?" her mother, Donna, asked when they got on the freeway.

"Nothing much." Jessie shrugged and glanced at Amber in the rearview mirror, happy that she was already dozing off. She checked on her mother out of the corner of her eye and saw she was watching her intently. "Lynn's in town. She's been staying with me at the house."

"Why?" Donna didn't sound disdainful, and Jessie fought the urge to get defensive. She didn't have anything to be defensive about—yet. "Doesn't she usually stay with her parents?"

"She does, yes." Jessie was quiet for a few moments, trying to calm her nerves. Was this the right time to tell her everything? Might as well get it over with. She opened her mouth, but nothing came out. She took a deep breath and cleared her throat. She lowered her voice in case Amber could still hear them, even though she appeared to be sleeping. "Wayne called when he got the divorce papers."

"Did he threaten you again?" Donna sounded angry now, and Jessie was still getting used to the woman her mother had become since her father died. The mama-bear-protecting-her-cubs routine was still a bit unnerving.

"Yes, he did. Karen wanted me to stay with her and Sarah, but I refuse to let Wayne run me out of my own house." She did her best to keep the extent of her fear out of her voice. She didn't want to worry her mother. "We compromised and decided Lynn would stay with me."

"That was nice of her. Of course she'll be leaving now that Amber's home, right?"

"Why would she?"

"Well, do you really think it's wise to have her there with Amber? I mean, she's a...a..." Jessie let her struggle with the word for a moment so she could compose herself enough to not lash out verbally. Donna finally gave up and sat back in her seat, staring out the side window.

"A lesbian, Mother?" Jessie was rather proud of the calmness in her voice. "Is that the word you were trying to say?"

"Yes." She refused to look away from the window. "Is it wise to have Amber around her?"

"Why? Karen's a lesbian. Sarah's a lesbian. They both spend time with Amber, so why on earth would it matter if Lynn did?"

"Because Karen is family. That's different." She looked down at her hands and then at Jessie.

Jessie was so angry that her vision actually wavered. She pulled off to the side of the freeway and put the car in Park before turning in her seat to face her mother. She glanced at Amber, who was still asleep.

"I'm only going to say this once, Mother. Being gay is not an illness. It isn't something you can catch simply by being around someone who is. It isn't something you learn, which should be pretty evident since Karen is gay and that certainly isn't how you and Dad raised her. It's something that you either are or you aren't. It's that simple. Amber will not turn out gay because she's surrounded by lesbians. That'll just cause her to become a more loving and understanding woman, because she won't be learning all the fear and hatred toward homosexuals that so many other people seem to teach their children."

Jessie stopped her tirade and sat back in her seat waiting for her mother to say something, but she was still staring out the window, her lips pressed firmly together and her hands fidgeting nervously in her lap.

"Are you going to say anything?"

"Please stop at the grocery store. I want to fix you dinner tonight."

"That's it?" Jessie put the car in gear and eased back out into traffic. "That's all you have to say?"

"I don't want to talk about it right now."

"Fine. But you can't fix me dinner, because Lynn's waiting for us at the house. I'm going to have dinner with her tonight."

"Then I'll fix dinner for both of you." Jessie looked over at her mother, who was now staring at her defiantly. "Is that a problem?"

"No." Jessie shrugged. What the heck was going on?

❖

Lynn stared at the tree she and Jessie had bought the day before and spent most of that morning decorating. She'd grinned when she saw the ornament she'd made for Jessie in the fourth grade. It was a silly little reindeer made out of old clothespins, and it surprised her to see it in Jessie's many boxes of ornaments. She'd have thought Jessie had thrown it out years ago.

The front door opened and she jumped up when Donna Greenfield walked in behind Jessie. She suddenly felt as if she were sixteen again and had done something wrong.

"Auntie Lynn!" Amber came running to her, and Lynn knelt and picked her up. "I missed you!"

"I missed you too, sweetie." Lynn hugged her and glanced over Amber's shoulder in Jessie's direction. "Did you have fun with your grandma?"

"Yes. Put me down. I got you a present."

"You did?" Amber tossed everything out of her suitcase looking for God only knew what. Finally she seized a bag with Mickey on it.

"Here." She thrust the bag out to Lynn. "Grandma said you'd like it."

Lynn was stunned. She'd always thought Jessie's mother simply tolerated her presence and, had it been up to her, would have banished Lynn from Jessie's life altogether.

"Open it. I want to see what it is." Jessie glanced at her mother, but Donna was watching Lynn with a strange expression.

Lynn removed a vintage Mickey Mouse T-shirt from the bag and held it up. She laughed at Amber, who was staring up at her with big brown eyes so much like her mother's.

"Do you like it?" she asked.

"I love it. Thank you, Amber." Lynn hugged her again, but Amber quickly ran back to her mother.

"Why don't you take her upstairs and get her unpacked," Donna suggested as she headed for the kitchen. "I'll start dinner."

"I'll help you with the suitcases," Lynn said.

"Lynn, I need your help in here. I'm sure Jessie can handle them."

Lynn took Jessie by the arm and led her over to the stairs, where she stopped and lowered her voice so no one could overhear her. "What the hell's going on?" She glanced back toward the kitchen.

"I have no clue. She wanted to fix dinner for us."

"Did you tell her about us?" Lynn really didn't want to go into the battlefield without all the information available.

"I just said that you're staying here with me. I swear, nothing came up about the two of us." Jessie kissed Lynn quickly. "I don't want to come back down here and find the two of you bonding over a beer or anything."

"Yeah, like that would ever happen." Lynn swallowed against a ball of tension and went back to the kitchen. "What can I do to help?"

Donna didn't answer right away, and Lynn was about to ask again, thinking maybe she hadn't heard her. Donna straightened and looked out into the living room before turning and facing Lynn. "I don't really need your help. I only wanted to talk to you."

"Okay." Lynn shifted her weight, uncomfortable with the way Donna was looking at her. She tried to get the conversation off to a good start. "Thank you for the shirt. You didn't have to do that."

"You had one like it when you were younger, didn't you?" She took a seat at the table, motioning for Lynn to do the same. "It must have been your favorite shirt, because it seemed like you wore it almost every day."

"It was." Lynn laughed in spite of her wariness. "I finally had to throw it away when it started to disintegrate."

Donna laughed too, and Lynn began to relax. She sat back in her chair and studied Donna, who appeared to be struggling with what she wanted to say.

"What are your intentions toward my daughter?" she finally asked.

Lynn continued to stare at her and finally decided she must have heard wrong. "Pardon me?"

"I asked you what your intentions are concerning Jessica."

Okay, so I did hear her right. Lynn looked away and glanced back toward the stairs, willing Jessie to come rescue her.

"If you can't answer a simple—"

"I love her," Lynn said, and met Donna's eyes again. If she wanted a fight, Lynn was ready for it. She would never hide her feelings for Jessie again. "I love Jessie with all that I am. I always have. If she'll let me, I want to spend the rest of my life with her."

Donna didn't speak at first, but held Lynn's gaze. After a moment, she nodded once, almost imperceptibly. "If I'd been stronger, I'd have left Arthur the first time he hit me. Also, I wouldn't have discouraged Jessica from following her heart, and maybe she would have found happiness with you long ago. I knew that you loved her when you girls were in high school. I did everything I could to keep Arthur from noticing it too, but that day when he caught the two of you hugging in the backyard..."

Lynn wasn't sure what to say. She sat still, aching to reach out to the woman who had always been an enigma. It had been painfully obvious that Arthur had run their household with the proverbial iron fist, and Donna really never had anything to say—about anything.

"I'm so sorry he hit you that day." Donna looked away and wiped at the tears that were rolling down her cheeks. "I should have said that long ago, but I was so scared of him. I hope to God you never have to know that kind of fear, Lynn. I hate myself for putting my girls through it, and for the fact that Jessica ended up marrying a man exactly like Arthur. I've often thought it would have been Jessie, not Karen, who grew up to be a lesbian. Jessie was always the tomboy, but you know that, don't you?"

Lynn smiled nervously, but decided not to interrupt Jessie's mother while she was in the mood to talk. Lynn couldn't remember ever hearing her so vocal. Thank God Arthur Greenfield had died.

"I was shocked when she told us she was getting married. Arthur was as happy as a clam that one of his girls had turned out 'normal.' I'll admit that I was delighted when we found out Jessica was pregnant." Donna looked away again, her eyes darting everywhere in the room except at Lynn. "I always wanted a grandchild. Amber's the most precious little girl in the world."

"Yes, she is." Lynn smiled at the memory of Amber running to her as soon as they'd walked in the door.

"She loves you, although I don't know how that's even possible when you're only around a few weeks a year. How does she even remember you from year to year, and at such a young age?"

"I guess I make an impression," Lynn said, trying to lighten the mood. She almost pulled her hand off the table when Donna reached for it, but let it remain. Donna squeezed her fingers gently.

"Jessie loves you too, Lynn. I've known that for years, even if she didn't realize it until now. And even if I don't fully understand it, I want Jessie to be happy. Sometimes you have to travel the long road in front of you to get to the destination that was right around the corner the whole time."

"Mrs. Greenfield—"

"Don't you think after so many years it's time to call me Donna? I've known you since you were Amber's age."

"Donna." Lynn smiled as she said it and took a deep breath. "It means a lot to me that you've said these things. I'm not as sure as you are that Jessie loves me, but I love Jessie and Amber, and I'll do everything in my power to make them happy, as long as they let me."

"Good. I was worried that Amber would get even more attached to you and then you'd leave. I think Jessie misunderstood me when I mentioned it. But, no matter." Donna stood, signaling that the conversation was finished. Lynn stood also, but she wasn't sure what she should do. Donna turned to her, a stern look on her face. "Just know that if you ever hurt her, you'll have me to answer to."

"Yes, ma'am."

"One more thing. I know you'll talk to Jessie about this, but I'd appreciate it if you'd wait until later—after I've gone home for the night."

CHAPTER TWENTY-ONE

I've been dying to find out what you and my mother talked about while I was upstairs," Jessie said after she'd taken Donna home and was sitting on the couch with Lynn. Amber was in bed for the night, and it was only the two of them, each holding a glass of wine.

"I'll bet you have." Lynn didn't say any more, and Jessie let out an exasperated sigh.

"You won't tell me?" Jessie took Lynn's wineglass and placed it on the coffee table next to her own. Lynn shook her head in response as Jessie pushed her onto her back, covering Lynn's body with her own. "I have ways of making you talk."

"I'm sure you have ways of making me do a lot of things."

It was obvious that Lynn was enjoying the game way too much. Jessie kissed the edge of her jaw before moving so she was sitting on the other end of the couch. She smiled when Lynn whimpered her protest. "She was warning you to stay away from me, wasn't she? Because Lynn is the big, bad lesbian who's going to pull me into her world."

Lynn grabbed Jessie's hand, pulling her back on top of her. "She wanted to know my intentions toward her daughter."

Jessie stared at her in disbelief, more than a little disoriented to think that her mother would accept the situation. Jessie was hurt on some level. Why wouldn't her mother have talked to her about it? She listened carefully as Lynn recounted the entire conversation.

"Seriously? She thought that *I* would be gay, and not Karen?"

Jessie got to her feet and began to pace back and forth in front of the coffee table.

"That's what she said."

"You're just messing with me, Lynn Patrick. My mother told you to keep your lesbian hands off me, didn't she?"

"My *lesbian hands*—that's funny." Lynn laughed when Jessie sat next to her again. "I'm telling the truth. She wants you to be happy, Jess. She knows that I love you, and she knows you love me. She's fine with this, as long as I don't hurt you."

Jessie looked at her skeptically, but finally shook her head. It would definitely take a while to get used to her mother's new understanding side.

❖

Jessie woke the next morning with a warm body against her back. She grinned lazily when Lynn's hand moved underneath her T-shirt to skim along her side. She tried to turn over, but another warm body was pressed against her front so she looked down. *Oh, shit.* Amber had gotten into the bed with them at some point during the night. How in the world was she going to explain this? Lynn had wanted to sleep in the guest room the night before, but Jessie had insisted it would be okay, because Amber knew not to come into her room without knocking and waiting to be invited in.

She turned her head toward Lynn as she grabbed her hand to stop it from moving to her breast. "We aren't alone," she whispered.

"What?" Lynn propped herself up on an elbow and looked over Jessie's body, her dismay evident. "I knew I shouldn't have slept in here."

"Stop." Jessie held her wrist when Lynn tried to get out of the bed. "It's too late now. She knows you're here, and it's pointless to move to the other room."

"Maybe it was too dark when she came in, and she didn't see me here."

"Lynn, stop. She'll find out sooner or later, so relax before you freak me out too." Jessie watched her intently until Lynn nodded, then she let go of Lynn's wrist and kissed Amber's head while she ran her fingers through her silky hair. It wasn't the way she'd wanted Amber to find out about them, and her heart was pounding. "Amber, honey. It's time to wake up now."

"Don't wanna." Amber stretched out but never opened her eyes.

"Honey, Mommy needs to get up. I need you to move so I can get out of the bed."

"Where's Daddy?"

Lynn stiffened behind her, but she reached back and placed a hand on her hip while searching for an appropriate answer. When she didn't reply right away Amber turned onto her side again and sighed. "Grandma says he's not coming home."

"He's not, sweetie." Jessie kissed her temple, then rested her forehead against Amber's shoulder. "Would it make you sad if he didn't live with us anymore?"

Amber shook her head, but didn't say anything. Jessie looked over at Lynn, who was listening to the conversation quietly.

"Do you miss him?" Jessie asked carefully.

"No. Daddy was mean. I'm glad he's gone."

"Honey, did Daddy ever hit you?" Jessie had asked her the same question before and Amber had said no, but that was when Wayne had still been living with them. If Amber had been afraid of him, she'd have said anything not to upset him. Jessie knew that, because she and Karen lived like that for most of their childhood.

"No. Daddy was mean to *you*. He made you cry. I don't like it when you cry. And he yelled all the time. If he's gone, then you don't cry no more, right, Mommy?" She looked at Jessie again, and when Jessie nodded, Amber smiled and threw the covers off. She faced the bed and smiled at Lynn. "Hi, Auntie Lynn. Are you gonna live with us now?"

"Would you like that, honey?" Jessie asked when she sensed Lynn's discomfort.

Amber nodded her head vigorously. "I love Auntie Lynn. She never makes you cry. And she plays with me."

With that, Amber ran out of the room, presumably to use the

bathroom or watch cartoons. Lynn let out a breath and fell onto her back, staring up at the ceiling. Jessie propped herself up on an elbow and put her hand in the center of Lynn's chest.

"It's that simple?" Lynn asked.

"She's six, Lynn. She has no idea *why* we're in the same bed." Jessie smiled at Lynn's obvious distress over the situation. "I probably don't need to explain it *all* to her right now."

"I haven't spent much time in the company of small children. It may take me some time to get used to this." Lynn pulled Jessie closer. "But make no mistake—I definitely want to get used to this."

"She adores you." Jessie kissed the tip of Lynn's nose. "Just like her mommy."

"Your mother brought up a good point last night. She wanted to know how Amber even remembers who I am when I'm not really here too often."

"I talk about you. A lot. And she absolutely loves to look at pictures. Believe it or not, she can pick you out of the crowd in your softball team picture in our senior yearbook." Jessie laid her head on Lynn's shoulder and began to play with the hem of Lynn's T-shirt as she spoke. "She's always asking me when you're coming to visit—even more often after Wayne left. I know it's crazy, but I think she instinctively knew not to talk about you when he was around."

"It's amazing the things that kids are in tune with, isn't it?" Lynn relaxed and let Jessie's hand work its way under her shirt.

"It is." Jessie kissed Lynn's neck, then pulled her hand away, even though she wanted to have her way with Lynn. "We have to go Christmas shopping, and Amber needs to sit on Santa's lap at some point. I can't believe Christmas is only a few days away."

"I know. Time flies, doesn't it?"

"It's flown since Saturday night. I could spend the rest of my life right here in your arms." Just as their lips touched, they heard Amber calling from downstairs.

"Mommy! I'm hungry!"

"A hungry kid would interrupt us every five minutes, though." Lynn seemed to try to stop laughing, but Jessie's scowl evidently made the situation even funnier. "I'm sorry. Let's make a date. Ten minutes after she goes to bed tonight, I'll meet you back here."

"We can lock the door." Jessie grinned as she got out of the bed. "I'll also have a little talk with Amber to remind her that Mommy's room is private, and she better knock."

"Jess? When we meet back here later...lose the T-shirt and sweatpants, all right?"

The words, the tone of voice, and the smoldering look in Lynn's eyes made her knees go weak. She hurried to the bathroom, trying to ignore her soaking panties.

CHAPTER TWENTY-TWO

Lynn's mother led Jessie and Amber around the living room on Christmas Eve, introducing them to various family members. It might have been a bit frigid outside, but unfamiliar warmth suffused Lynn. This undeniable feeling of happiness made her sigh with contentment.

"Thank you for inviting me to share Christmas Eve with you and your family," Jessie's mother said.

"You *are* part of the family." Lynn kissed her cheek, which caused her to blush. If someone had told Lynn a week earlier she'd kiss Donna Greenfield, she'd have laughed.

"Thank you. I've lived across the street from your parents for over twenty-five years, and they've never been anything but kind. It's my fault we never became better friends."

"No, it was your husband's fault." Lynn expected Donna to argue the point, which she would have if her husband was still alive, but she just nodded.

"Yes, it was. But he's gone, and I really don't want to think about him anymore. I wasted so much time protecting him." Donna looked across the room at Jessie and Amber and smiled. "I'm so glad Jessica had the sense to get out of her marriage when she did. I hate to think she could have ended up like I did—so used to the abuse that I never thought twice about it." She placed a hand on Lynn's forearm. "I never thanked you for standing up to him, did I?"

"No, ma'am. I don't think he would have been happy about it if you had."

"You scared the heck out of him, you know." At Lynn's look of disbelief, Donna laughed. "I don't think he ever expected anyone to defy him, much less a woman."

"Much less a sixteen-year-old girl."

Donna nodded as she saluted Lynn with the drink she held. "He left Jessie alone after that." Her voice dropped a level or two, and Lynn had to move closer to hear what she was saying. "He thought you were just unstable enough to follow through on your threat. I knew you only did it to protect Jessica, though. This is coming years too late, but thank you, Lynn. Thank you for caring enough about my little girl to do what you did."

Lynn smiled but didn't know what to say. Luckily her father arrived at that moment and spared her the awkward silence.

"Donna, did you bring those delicious cookies you promised Rose you were going to make?" he asked.

"Oh, shoot. I left them sitting on the kitchen table. I'll run across the street and get them." Donna headed for the hall closet to grab her coat, but Lynn stopped her.

"I can do it," she offered, reaching around Donna for her own jacket. She had it on before Donna could think of protesting. She handed Lynn her keys and thanked her three times before Lynn finally made it out the door.

Lynn stood on the front porch for a moment, her breath coming out in puffs of winter mist as she remembered all the fun times that she, Jessie, Charlie, and Karen had while growing up. The old birch tree they used to climb was still there next to the house, the one Charlie fell out of and broke his arm. He'd told their father Lynn had pushed him, but Robert hadn't believed him. Lynn smiled at the memory and shook her head. Charlie had always been trying to get her into trouble.

She walked down the driveway but stopped when a car pulled into Donna's driveway. She hung back and thought her heart might stop when Wayne got out of the car. She crouched next to her grandmother's Chevy and kept an eye on him. When he knocked on the front door, Lynn closed her eyes and clenched her fists, trying to keep her nerves from fraying.

He pounded on the door for a few minutes and kept looking over his shoulder at Lynn's house, making her worry that he'd come there looking for Donna. Thank God they'd brought Lynn's car and left Jessie's car at her house. If he'd seen her car, he'd have definitely come looking for her.

Finally, he went back to his car and got in, but he didn't leave. Lynn was plotting how to get back up the driveway without him noticing her when he jumped out of the car again. He stuck a scrap of paper between the storm door and the front door, then slammed back into his car and screeched away from the house.

Lynn sat on the ground and rested her head back against the car until she began to breathe again. The driveway was cold on her rear end, but she barely noticed. Should she tell Jessie? Should she tell anyone? Should she pretend she never saw him?

She remembered the cookies she was on her way to get. She'd never be able to *not* read the note he'd left, and once she did, she wouldn't be able to keep it to herself. She stood, brushed off her butt, and walked across the street.

❖

"What took you so long?" Rose asked when Lynn finally walked into the kitchen carrying a huge tray of cookies.

"I got lost." Lynn forced a smile. She glanced around at the people in the kitchen before gazing back at her mother. "Where's Jessie?"

"Your grandmother cornered her and is showing her all your embarrassing baby pictures. I told her Jessie's probably already seen them all, but she insisted and said Amber had never seen them. Amber, however, is playing in the spare bedroom with her cousins."

Lynn was barely listening, and when Karen walked into the room, Lynn grabbed her arm and dragged her into the garage.

"What are you doing?" Karen asked when they were alone.

"Wayne's here."

"Here? As in at this party?"

"No." Lynn raked her fingers through her hair. "I went across the street to get your mother's cookies, and he was in the driveway."

"Are you sure it was him?"

Rather than frustrate herself further, Lynn pulled the note out of her pocket and thrust it toward Karen. As Karen read it she couldn't help but think of Wayne's words, since she'd read it a hundred times already.

Donna,

Please tell Jessie I need to speak to her. I'm so terribly sorry I hurt her. You have to know I never meant to do that. I know we could work things out if she would just agree to talk to me. I'll be in town for a couple of days, but then I have to go back to Nevada. Please have her call me.

Wayne

"Fuck," Karen said, and that single word summed it all up. Karen crumpled the paper but then smoothed it out and read it again. "Fuck."

Lynn walked to her father's work bench and sat down, putting her head in her hands.

"We can't tell her," Karen said.

"Are you crazy? We have to." Lynn shook her head and placed both hands on her knees. "I'd do anything to protect Jessie, especially from a scumbag like Wayne, but not telling her he's in town would be a huge mistake."

"He'll only be here for a few days. We can keep her away from the house for that long. He won't know where to find her."

"Really? He's been to your mother's, and you'd have to be dense to think he hasn't been to your house already. I'm surprised he didn't come over here." Lynn stood and began pacing, but Karen placed a hand on her forearm, stopping her.

"What are you two doing out here?" Jessie asked. Lynn and Karen exchanged glances, but neither of them said anything. Jessie's eyes settled on Karen's hand on Lynn's arm, and Lynn pulled away from her. "Lynn? What's going on?"

"Nothing going on," Karen said. She stuffed the note in Lynn's jacket pocket. "Where's Sarah?"

Lynn cursed under her breath when Karen walked into the house, leaving her to decide whether to tell Jessie. She met Jessie's eyes and motioned for her to have a seat on the workbench. Lynn sat next to her, struggling with how to begin.

"Lynn, talk to me. Tell me what's happening."

"I went to get something from your mother's house, and..." She wasn't sure she could actually say the words. She took the note from her pocket and placed it on her leg, smoothing it out with both palms. Having something to occupy her hands helped loosen her tongue. "Wayne was there. He left this for your mother."

Jessie took the note with shaking hands that had nothing to do with how cold it was in the garage. Lynn waited patiently for Jessie to read it, but was surprised when Jessie folded it up and put it in her back pocket as she stood.

"We're missing the party."

"Jess, that's all you have to say?"

"What do you want me to say? I'm not going to call him, and he'll be back in Nevada soon. I have a restraining order against him, so if he comes near me, I can have him arrested." Jessie's smile was forced. Lynn wanted nothing more than to hold her in her arms and make all the ugliness in her life go away. "Let me guess—Karen didn't want you to tell me about this."

"She only wanted to protect you."

"And what about you?"

"I want to protect you too." Lynn put a hand on Jessie's cheek, rubbing her thumb over the scar beneath Jessie's eye. She quelled the anger that threatened to rise again at the thought of anyone hurting Jessie. "But I don't think shielding you from the truth is the way to go about it. It's better that you know he's here, because if he does manage to get in touch with you, he won't catch you off guard."

"Thank you." Jessie relaxed into Lynn's touch briefly before threading her fingers through Lynn's hair to pull her close for a kiss.

"I decided to get involved with you in spite of his threats. I can't let him run my life any longer, Lynn. I wish he wasn't a part of my life, but—he's Amber's father."

For a moment, Lynn panicked, thinking perhaps Jessie *would* contact him, but Jessie shook her head as if reading her mind.

"I don't want to talk to him, Lynn. I want him to go back to Nevada and leave me the hell alone."

"Leave *us* the hell alone." Lynn pulled her close and held her for a few moments. No matter how much she wanted to protect Jessie, she didn't have a clue how to. And that realization terrified her.

CHAPTER TWENTY-THREE

Jessie tried to make the next few days as normal as possible for Amber—at least as normal as it could be when they didn't spend Christmas in their own house. Amber was a smart kid, and Jessie hated lying, but she didn't see any other choice. Wayne knew that Lynn's family lived across the street from Jessie's mother, but he had no reason to think Jessie would be there, since she'd never spent time there in the past. That was Rose and Robert's take on the situation anyway, and why they'd offered to let Jessie and Amber stay with them. If he did show up there, Charlie had offered his place as a refuge. Jessie didn't know what she would do without the Patrick family in her corner.

"Mommy?" Amber said from her chair at the desk in the corner of Lynn's old room. Jessie diverted her gaze to her feet and touched her hand.

"What is it, baby?"

"How come we aren't home? When can we go home?"

"Don't you like it here?" Jessie sighed. Amber had been asking these same questions every day since Christmas, and tomorrow was New Year's Eve. Jessie still didn't have a good reason to give her, other than the truth, and Amber was far too young to have to deal with adult problems.

"Yes, but..." Amber looked out the window. "How will I get to school?"

"Is that what you're worried about?"

Amber nodded. "I missed some to go to Florida, but I can go back, right? I want to see my friends."

"Hopefully we'll be home before you have to go to school, baby. You've still got a few days." Jessie motioned for her to come and sit with her on the bed, and Amber got onto her lap rather than beside her. A tear rolled down Jessie's cheek when Amber put her arms around her neck and rested her head on Jessie's shoulder. She gently stroked Amber's hair as she rocked slightly.

"I love you, Mommy." Amber's arms tightened, and Jessie couldn't stop the sob that escaped her. Amber leaned back and looked into her face. "Why are you crying? You only cry when Daddy gets mad at you."

"I'm just happy that you love me." Jessie smiled and brushed away her tears. "And I love you too."

"Why cry when you're happy?" Amber crinkled her nose and got off Jessie's lap. "You should laugh when you're happy, not cry."

"I couldn't agree more." Lynn's voice coming from the doorway startled Jessie, but the softness of Lynn's tone warmed her.

"Then what would you suggest we do about that?" Jessie asked.

"Well, I was thinking maybe dinner at the Spaghetti Factory and a movie." Lynn smiled when Amber looked up with an expression of pure joy.

"Can we, Mommy?" she asked with a pleading look. "Please?"

Jessie held her hand out to Lynn, who sat next to her on the bed. She loved that Lynn was trying to help Amber forget they were living in a strange house. She also loved that Amber was so enamored with Lynn.

"That sounds like a wonderful idea." Jessie held onto Lynn's hand as she turned her attention to Amber. "Why don't you get cleaned up so we can go?"

Lynn squeezed Jessie's hand while Amber ran out of the room and down the hall to the bathroom. Jessie kissed Lynn on the cheek.

"What was that for?"

"For distracting her." Jessie placed a hand on Lynn's cheek. "You're so good with her, and she loves you."

"I love her too. She's a great kid." Lynn kissed Jessie's palm. "And I love her mother too."

"Have I told you how amazing you are?"

"Not today, no." Lynn grinned, and the glint in her eye caused Jessie to blush because she had indeed told her that the night before. Lynn took mercy on her, though, by changing the subject. "Karen called a few minutes ago."

"Has something happened?" Jessie turned serious, all thoughts of the previous evening's activities gone. Normally Karen would have called Jessie's cell phone, but Jessie had turned it off the day after Christmas because Wayne was trying to contact her on it ten times a day. Karen and Sarah had been staying at Jessie's house, waiting to see if Wayne would show up there, but so far he hadn't.

"No, and Karen's beginning to think he's probably gone back to Vegas."

"What do you think?"

"If he was still here, he'd have tried to see you."

Jessie chewed on her bottom lip, trying to think like Wayne. He'd gone to Vegas to do some work for a friend, and that project wasn't supposed to be completed until mid-January. He'd already lost one job because of his brush with the law, and she really didn't think he'd be willing to risk losing another one.

"You're probably right." Jessie relaxed a little for the first time since Lynn told her she'd seen him. "Let's go out and enjoy ourselves for the evening, and forget about him."

"That sounds good to me." Lynn stood, holding a hand out to Jessie.

Jessie hoped that they *were* right. It would be nice to move back into her own home.

❖

"Amber's sound asleep." Lynn redirected her gaze to Jessie in the passenger seat next to her. "I enjoyed tonight."

"So did I. Amber loves the Spaghetti Factory. Thank you for suggesting it." Jessie appeared as though she wanted to say more, but instead looked down at her hands in her lap.

"What is it?" Lynn prodded gently. She placed two fingers under Jessie's chin, turning her head until their eyes met. "What's wrong?"

"I'm a little worried about what'll happen when Wayne comes back from Nevada for good."

Lynn wanted to address her concerns, but really didn't think sitting in the car, in her parents' driveway, was the place to have the conversation. She kissed Jessie quickly on the lips, then motioned to the backseat.

"How about we get her inside and into bed, then sit down and talk about that?" Jessie nodded, and Lynn jumped out so she could get Amber out of the back. She carried her up to the bedroom, then left Jessie to tuck her in while Lynn went downstairs to the kitchen, where her mother was waiting for her.

"You two are going out tomorrow night, right?" Rose asked.

"No, we decided to stay in. I thought I told you that."

"You did, but I spoke with Donna while you were at the movie. Karen's convinced that Wayne is gone."

"So are we," Jessie said as she came in and sat next to Lynn. She looked back and forth between them. "Why are we talking about Wayne?"

"I was trying to tell Lynn that you two should go out and have fun tomorrow night. It's New Year's Eve, and you should celebrate." Rose stood, indicating that it was decided. "I won't take no for an answer."

"We'd never find a babysitter on such short notice."

"You have a problem with Robert and me?" Rose winked. "I have a pizza and movie party planned for the three of us. I'll even let Amber try to stay up until midnight."

Lynn laughed, and when Jessie looked at her, she held up her hands defensively. "Mother has spoken. It would not be wise to defy her, trust me."

"I did raise you well, didn't I?" Rose kissed Lynn on the cheek before heading upstairs to bed.

"I guess that's settled." Jessie chuckled.

"It most definitely is." Lynn studied Jessie's profile. It still amazed her that she was so close to living her dream of being with Jessie forever. If only they didn't have to deal with Wayne Paulson and everything that went along with the unstable asshole. Lynn took a deep breath. "I'm going back to San Francisco the day after New Year's. I have to pack my things and arrange for my loft to be sold, which shouldn't be too hard, because my friend Bri has been begging me to sell it to her for months. I should only be gone a few days, and I'll definitely be back before Wayne's supposed to return. But I want you to come with me."

"I can't, Lynn. Amber missed two weeks of school before their winter break, and I can't let her be absent any more. I'd love to go with you, but I can't."

"I worry about you here alone."

"I know. Your mom's already said we could stay here while you're gone."

"She did?" Her mother hadn't mentioned it to her. She was happy her parents were looking out for Jessie and Amber.

"We'll be okay until you get back." Jessie pulled Lynn's hand into her lap and slowly ran her thumb along the back of it, causing a ripple of pleasure to run through her. "You're coming to live with us, right?"

"If that's what you want." Lynn was hesitant, because they hadn't discussed it. She hadn't wanted to assume anything, but had decided to move back to the area so she could see where their relationship was going.

"Why wouldn't I want that? We've wasted enough time. You're more important to me than I can say, Lynn. You always have been, and if I'd been more in tune with my feelings, I'd have realized it years ago."

"What about Wayne?"

"He's definitely a problem." Jessie closed her eyes and shook her head. "I honestly don't know what to expect from him, but I don't want to let him control me any longer. He and I both need to start out fresh."

"Then I'd be more than happy to live with you." Lynn squeezed her hand. "I can't imagine *not* being with you."

"Good. Then that's settled."

Lynn truly wanted to believe everything was in place, but she didn't. Wayne would never let them be. From what little she knew about him, the man wasn't likely to lose gracefully, especially to a woman.

CHAPTER TWENTY-FOUR

Lynn was happy they'd decided to go out. They'd just finished dancing to the fourth song in a row, and she sat down at their table, pulling Jessie into her lap with a laugh. Jessie's arms went around Lynn's neck, and Lynn pulled her closer for a kiss.

"Jesus, don't you two ever stop?" Karen asked from her seat on the other side of the table. "Maybe you should get a room somewhere."

"Oh, please—tell me you and Sarah weren't like this when you first got together." Jessie laughed as she extricated herself from Lynn's grasp and took her own chair. Lynn grabbed the bottom of it and pulled her as close as the chairs would allow before putting her arm around Jessie's shoulders.

"That's beside the point." Karen chuckled. "And who says we aren't still like that?"

Unfortunately, Sarah had to work, but she kept stealing a minute or two when she could to sit with the three of them. It was almost midnight, and people were getting their glasses of champagne and preparing for the countdown. Lynn kissed Jessie again, but before it became steamy, a hand on her shoulder pulled her and Jessie apart.

"What the hell?" Lynn said when Sarah bent close so they could both hear her.

"Wayne's here." She tilted her head in the direction of the front doors before sitting next to Karen.

Jessie looked where Sarah had indicated and moved her chair

away from Lynn's quickly. When Jessie glanced at Lynn, the fear in Jessie's eyes terrified her.

"We have to call the police," Karen said, reaching for her cell phone.

Sarah grabbed her arm. "I already did. They're on their way."

Lynn was still close enough to Jessie that she could hear her quietly swearing. Wayne stood only a few feet away. Lynn tried to take Jessie's hand under the table, but Jessie jerked it away.

"What the fuck are you doing in a place like this?" he bellowed loud enough that most of the people around them turned to see what was happening. "I went by the house and you weren't there. I should have known you'd be here with your dyke friends."

"Wayne, you can't be here," Jessie said calmly.

"I saw you kissing her." He pointed at Lynn, then looked accusingly at Jessie again. "I knew this was why you kicked me out and want a divorce now. You're a fucking dyke!"

Lynn stood impulsively, because if she'd taken the time to think about it, she'd have kept her butt in the chair. She got close enough to him that she was in his face, but was careful not to touch him. Karen and Jessie both were trying to get her to back down, but she refused to budge.

"She left you because you beat the shit out of her and put her in the hospital," Lynn told him, not even trying to hide her hatred. She'd love to punch him but managed to restrain herself. "She left you because you're an asshole."

Lynn was dimly aware that the music had stopped playing and now everyone was watching them in shocked silence. Apparently a domestic dispute was more interesting than the New Year's Eve celebration. The lights were being turned up as well, but Lynn was so focused on the man in front of her she barely noticed.

"I knew you were sleeping with her," Wayne said with a sneer. His words were directed at Jessie, which only made Lynn angrier. He looked at Lynn again, and she smelled the whiskey on his breath. "Have you two been fucking around since high school? Is that what you do when you come to visit every year? This is all starting to make sense now."

"The police are on their way," Lynn informed him, choosing to ignore his asinine attempts to provoke her. "I'd suggest you get the hell out of here before they come haul your ass away."

He took a step back and looked her up and down, shaking his head in disgust.

"What are you, her knight in shining armor?" he asked with a laugh. He suddenly turned serious as he confronted Lynn. She didn't flinch or give ground. "Jessica is *my* wife, and *I'm* not going anywhere, bitch. You're certainly welcome to try and make me, though."

He shoved her hard with both hands, and Lynn fell over the chair she'd been sitting in earlier. Sarah went to her side to make sure she was all right, but Lynn shoved her hand away and tried to get back on her feet. Wayne started to walk toward her, but Jessie stuck her foot out into his path, and he fell face-first onto the ground a couple of feet away. He landed hard, but almost immediately pulled himself back up, glaring at Jessie with hatred in his eyes.

"Get off me!" Lynn yelled at Sarah when she tried again to help her. Lynn watched helplessly when Wayne stepped close to Jessie and obviously said something to her, because Jessie's eyes flared in fear as she backed away from him.

"Come on, tough guy," an authoritative voice said, and a uniformed arm reached for Wayne. The cop was looking at Jessie. "Are you all right, Jess?"

Jessie only nodded before going to stand next to Karen. Lynn finally allowed Sarah to help her to her feet, went to Jessie, and tried to put an arm around her waist, but Jessie pulled away. The rejection stung, but Lynn told herself it was simply because Wayne was still watching her.

"What happened here?" the officer asked. Lynn thought he looked familiar, but didn't have time to think about where she might have seen him before. He glanced at the awkward way Lynn was holding her hand, then met her eyes. "Do you need medical attention?"

"No."

"Look around, Officer," Wayne said as the cop handcuffed him.

"We're in the middle of a den of iniquity, and *I'm* the one you're going to arrest?"

"Well, sir," the cop said with mock concern. "The last time I checked, it isn't illegal to be gay—as much as some people would like it to be. However, it *is* illegal to violate a restraining order so, yes, *you* are the one that I'm arresting. You have the right to remain silent…"

Lynn tuned him out, vaguely aware of a sharp pain in her wrist but more concerned with Jessie's well-being. She picked up the chair she had fallen over and helped Jessie sit down, then knelt in front of her.

"Jess, are you okay?" she asked, while Sarah began pushing people away from them. Lynn held her left arm close to her chest and put her right hand gently on Jessie's thigh. A second officer had taken Wayne from the building, and the first one crouched next to Lynn.

"He'll at least spend the night in jail, Jess," he said, taking one of Jessie's hands in his own.

Lynn looked at him and and finally recognized him. "Mike?" she asked in disbelief. He nodded in her direction, obviously pleased that she'd remembered. "My God, Mike, I haven't seen you in years."

Mike Williams had been her boyfriend in high school. Her *gay* boyfriend. The fake relationship had saved both of them from a lot of ridicule and questions. She remembered Jessie telling her he'd become a cop, but Lynn hadn't seen or talked to him since graduation.

"Jess, do you have a ride home?" he asked, redirecting his attention to Jessie.

"She came with me," Lynn answered. "I'll take her home."

Mike glanced at the wrist she was holding tight to her body and shook his head. He met her eyes. "You really should have that examined, Lynn. It looks broken."

"I'm fine." She wasn't in the mood to have people telling her what she should do. She turned her attention back to Jessie, and Mike stood to speak with Karen and Sarah before he finally left.

"I want to go home," Jessie said after a moment. Lynn nodded and started to get to her feet, but Jessie looked pointedly at her sister. "Will you take me, please?"

Lynn glanced at Karen in confusion, but she appeared to be just as confused as Lynn.

Sarah was talking to one of the other bartenders, then made her way back over to Lynn.

"Come on," she said, taking hold of Lynn's uninjured arm. "I'm driving you to the hospital so you can have that wrist x-rayed. It really does look like it's broken."

"No, I'm taking Jessie home."

"No," Jessie said, tears in her eyes and a wounded expression on her face. Lynn wanted nothing more than to ease her pain. "I need to be alone right now. Go get your wrist taken care of and I'll talk to you tomorrow."

Lynn stared in disbelief. Sarah brought her some ice to put on her wrist, and they watched Karen and Jessie walk out the door.

"What the hell just happened?" Lynn was in a daze as she walked beside Sarah out to her car. She reached into her pocket with her right hand and pulled out her keys. After pushing the button to unlock the doors, she tossed them to Sarah.

"Honestly—I'm not sure, honey." Sarah got in and started the car. "She probably needs some time to sort things out."

Lynn closed her eyes and rested her head back against the seat. She was suddenly aware of the sharp pain in her wrist and winced as she tried to convince herself Jessie's reaction to the events was normal for a woman whose estranged and abusive husband had shown up out of the blue. *Please, let that be what it is.*

Chapter Twenty-five

It was almost four in the morning when Sarah pulled into the driveway. Lynn opened her eyes slowly and took in her surroundings, realizing they were in front of Sarah's house.

"Why didn't you just take me home?" Lynn shook her head, trying to get the cobwebs out. She was a little loopy from the drugs they'd given her in the emergency room before setting her wrist, which was broken in two places. She was grateful she could at least still type with her right hand. It would be slow going, but doable.

"I wouldn't have a way to get home, Lynn." Sarah put the car in Park and shut off the lights. "Also, I didn't see any reason to wake your parents up at this time of the morning."

Lynn could hear the agitation in her voice, and she turned her head to look at her. The world around her began to swim, and she had to close her eyes. She felt as if she'd been drinking for three days straight. "What the hell did they give me?" she asked.

"I don't know, but whatever it was, it's really fucking with you. You keep asking the same questions, but that's only when you haven't fallen asleep in the middle of a word." Lynn opened one eye and tried to focus on Sarah. "The doctor said you'd probably be out of it for a few hours. We need to get you inside so you can sleep this off."

Lynn didn't want to move. She was about to tell Sarah to leave her in the car when the passenger side door opened and Sarah was pulling her out, with Karen standing right outside the front door, obviously waiting for them. Lynn concentrated on walking the few steps from the car without falling.

"I guess it's broken?" Karen asked. She took Lynn's other arm and they both helped her into the living room.

"In two places." Lynn held up two fingers to emphasize the fact and laughed shakily. "Have you ever broken anything? It hurts like hell. But, you know, they gave me some awesome painkillers. Makes it almost tolerable."

"I'll bet it does. Do you want anything to drink?"

"Beer."

"One water, coming right up," Sarah said as she went straight to the kitchen. She returned after a moment with a bottle of spring water and handed it to Lynn before sitting next to her.

"You should talk to your distributor," Lynn said seriously, wrinkling her nose after she took a swig. "This beer is really watered down."

Karen and Sarah laughed, and Lynn looked back and forth between them, wondering what was so funny about watered-down beer. She glanced over to the front hall and saw a duffel bag sitting near the front door.

"Is that mine?" she asked, and her heart dropped. It was the bag she'd left at Jessie's when they went to stay at her parents' house.

"Lynn—"

"Come on," Sarah said as she tried to get her to her feet again. "Let's get you to bed, and we can talk about it in the morning."

"That *is* mine." Lynn pulled her arm out of Sarah's grip and looked at Karen, but she was still having trouble focusing. "Why's it here?"

"Jessie's had second thoughts," Karen said, and glanced over Lynn's shoulder at Sarah.

"About what?" Lynn was dazed, and it wasn't just from the pills. She felt as though someone had reached into her chest and ripped her heart out. She shook her head slowly. "I don't understand."

"Lynn." Karen hesitated again. "Things were moving too fast for her. She said to tell you she's sorry. She loves you as a friend, but she said she can't do this anymore. She has Amber to think about."

"I need to talk to her." Lynn stood on unsteady legs and dug in her pocket for her keys but finally realized that Sarah hadn't given them back to her. Sarah gripped her good wrist and urged her to sit again.

"You're not doing anything tonight. You're doped up, and even if you weren't, it's four o'clock. Sleep a few hours, and maybe you can talk to her in the morning."

"I thought she could love me," Lynn said, more to herself than to anyone else. She wanted to cry, but hadn't she expected it to happen? Had she really thought Jessie could be happy with her? "I believed that she wanted to give us a try. I should have known that this was all too good to be true. Lynn Patrick just isn't meant to be happy. Jessie's the only woman I've ever loved, did you know that?"

Karen sat next to her on the couch and put her arm around her, pulling her over so Lynn's head rested on her shoulder. She stroked her hand through Lynn's hair as she spoke to her. "I'm so sorry about all this, Lynn. I know you love her, and I know how hard this must be for you. It is what Jessie wants, though, and it might be for the best. She said she was worried you wanted more from her than she could give right now. Just let her have some space for a while and maybe she'll change her mind."

"How long does she expect me to wait?" Lynn asked irritably. She wished the pain meds they'd given her at the hospital would dull the ache in her chest. "I was going to move up here so that we could be together—so she wouldn't have to uproot Amber and leave her family."

"Three weeks ago she was straight," Sarah pointed out quietly. "You were her first, Lynn. You know those relationships hardly ever work out."

"This was different. She knew what she wanted."

"How can you be so sure?" Sarah asked.

"People change their minds," Karen added.

Lynn turned to look at her, trying to keep the room from spinning. "No, she told me just last night she wanted me to move in with her. That she'd never been more certain of anything. She came out to your mother, for God's sake. Is that something that you do if you're not sure? If you're having second thoughts?"

Apparently neither of them had a response. Hot tears rolled down Lynn's cheeks. *Shit, maybe she* is *gay, and she's decided it isn't me she wants. She never actually said she loved me in that way. I'm such a fucking fool.* Lynn wiped at the tears angrily, determined to get the thoughts out of her head.

"Babe, why don't you go on to bed," Sarah said to Karen. "I'll get her situated in the spare room and be up in a minute."

Karen nodded and stood up, but took Sarah into the kitchen to talk to her. They stood in the doorway, obviously to keep an eye on her, and Lynn chuckled humorlessly. It wasn't as though she could go anywhere without her keys. She strained to hear their conversation.

"Jessie doesn't want to talk to her," Karen said. "I'll explain it all to you after she leaves in the morning."

Lynn felt as if someone had stabbed her in the heart. She couldn't deal with any more of it tonight. They were right—she needed to sleep for a few hours, and maybe she could convince Jessie to talk to her in the morning.

"You ready to go to bed?" Sarah asked after Karen had disappeared up the stairs.

Lynn nodded, not really caring if she slept in a bed or right there on the couch, or even on the floor. Sarah helped her stand and handed her a couple of pills. Lynn vaguely remembered the ER nurse giving them to Sarah in order to help her sleep. She took them without question and allowed Sarah to lead her upstairs.

"Will you stay here with me for a little bit?" Lynn was sitting on the bed, and Sarah had been about to walk out the door. Lynn held up her injured hand. "I don't think I can undress myself with this cast on."

Sarah nodded and then disappeared, but soon came back carrying Lynn's duffel bag. Sarah untied and removed Lynn's shoes, then began to unbutton her blouse.

"I'm sorry." Lynn began to cry again, and Sarah sat next to her, resting one hand lightly on Lynn's thigh. "I don't know what the hell happened tonight, Sarah. My entire world just fell apart."

"If you give her a little time, Jessie'll come around."

"I've spent so long hoping that someday she and I might get together. I'm thirty-three years old, Sarah. If she really wants this to be over, I have to try to make a new life, don't I?"

Sarah sighed and nodded slowly. Sarah couldn't tell her what she wanted to hear, but Lynn had been wishing she'd have at least given her some kind of hope.

"Get some sleep," Sarah told her. "I'll see you in the morning."

After Sarah left, she managed to maneuver herself so she was lying properly on the bed. She stared at the ceiling, willing her mind to shut down, but eventually the pills did their job and she drifted into an uneasy sleep.

CHAPTER TWENTY-SIX

L ynn woke the next morning to the unrelenting pain in her wrist and an intense ache in her chest. Her breath caught when the memories of the previous night came crashing back. The sun was shining in on her face, and she glanced at the bedside clock. Noon. The need to pee was overwhelming, so she got up, barely managing to get a few buttons on her blouse done before she grabbed her toothbrush and headed for the bathroom.

When she finished, she struggled to tuck her blouse in with one hand, which proved to be more difficult than brushing her teeth had been. She splashed some water on her face, then ran her wet fingers through her hair.

She returned to the bedroom on autopilot, picked up her bag, and headed downstairs. No one was around, so she dropped the duffel by the door, walked into the kitchen, and stopped. There sat Jessie at the table with Karen and Sarah. Karen tapped Sarah on the arm and motioned toward the door.

"Hi, Auntie Lynn!" Amber ran to her, and Lynn crouched to greet her, trying desperately not to cry. The fantasy Lynn had harbored of her and Jessie over the years had never included the little girl, but Lynn had fallen for Amber too. She hugged Amber with her good arm and kissed her on the cheek. Amber placed a gentle hand on her cast and looked at her with concern. "What happened?"

"I fell and hurt myself." Lynn forced a smile before Sarah took Amber's hand to lead her out of the room. Lynn stood and met Sarah's eyes for a moment.

"There's coffee if you want some," Sarah murmured.

Jessie refused to look at Lynn. If she did, her resolve would break. Without a word, she got up, poured Lynn a cup of coffee, and put cream and sugar into it. She finally met Lynn's eyes when she placed the cup in front of her. The pain that greeted her broke her heart. The broken wrist wasn't all that hurt her.

"Can we talk for a moment?" she asked, completely unsure of Lynn's reaction. She took a deep breath to steady her nerves.

"According to what Karen told me last night, we really don't have anything to talk about." Lynn took a seat, then a sip from her coffee. "She made it sound as if you've already made up your mind."

"How's your wrist?" Jessie looked at the cast and glanced away again when tears threatened. *God damn Wayne for thoroughly fucking up my life.*

"Broken," Lynn replied, with a shrug.

"Does it hurt much?"

"I've had worse pain." She paused, but when Jessie refused to look at her, she went on. "What did I do to fuck this up, Jess? I admit that I don't know much about relationships, but I thought things were going pretty well."

"You didn't do anything to fuck it up, Lynn. It was me. I'm not ready for this." Jessie looked away, knowing that if she allowed Lynn to hold her gaze, she'd give in. "You're going back to San Francisco now, and I thought this would be the best time to end it. I just got out of a bad marriage. Actually, I'm still in the middle of ending it. I'm sorry, but I'm not sure I'm in the right state of mind to jump into a new situation. We were moving too fast. I need to be alone with Amber for a while."

"I was only going back to get my things. I was planning to move up here and live with you, remember? You told me that was what you wanted. Is this because of what Wayne did last night? I can take care of myself, Jessie. Don't let him force us apart."

"It has nothing to do with Wayne." The words, the blatant lie, tasted like metal in her mouth. Jessie hated herself, but she knew it was for the best. At least she'd been convinced without Lynn sitting in front of her. But in the cold morning light, with Lynn across the table from her, she wasn't entirely sure anymore. "Lynn, I don't want to lose you as a friend, but I can't give you what you want right now. Maybe I can someday, but not right now. Please, tell me you understand."

"I can't do that, because I *don't* understand. And you have no idea what I want, so don't give me that crap about not being able to give it to me." Lynn shook her head, pushed her coffee cup away, and stood. "I hope you don't expect me to wait around forever for you to realize you're making the biggest mistake of your life."

She turned and left the kitchen, not giving Jessie the opportunity to respond.

"What happened?" Sarah asked when Lynn walked into the living room.

"Just give me my damn keys so I can go home." Sarah handed them to her and she put them in her pocket. "I'm leaving now. Thank you for the hospitality and for the ride to and from the hospital."

"I went out this morning and got this filled for you." Sarah handed her a bottle of the pain pills the doctor had prescribed the night before.

Lynn looked at it blankly before putting it in her jacket pocket. She picked up her bag, then glanced back toward the kitchen.

Jessie had been standing there watching her and crying, but Lynn squared her shoulders and walked out the door without looking back.

"Are you sure you did the right thing?"

"No, Karen, I'm not sure." Jessie brushed the tears from her face and went to sit on the couch with her. "I love her so much."

"Then go stop her, for God's sake. *Tell* her." Sarah looked back and forth between them, and Jessie began to cry again. "Is somebody going to tell me what's going on here?"

Jessie looked at Karen for help, but got only a cold stare. Obviously Karen didn't really understand either.

"I don't feel right involving her in my domestic turmoil," Jessie said after a moment.

"You're kidding me, right?" Sarah laughed before she sat down in the chair opposite the couch. "Jesus, Jessie, she's already *involved*. Why didn't you just tell her the truth instead of making her feel like shit? She loves you more than life itself. I can't believe you took it upon yourself to make this decision without her."

"I did it *for* her, Sarah," Jessie said in her own defense. She felt attacked for giving up the only thing in her life with any meaning other than her daughter. "He broke her wrist. What if he did something worse? Last night, he whispered in my ear that he'd kill her if he ever saw us together again. I don't know if he really would, but I'd never be able to live with myself if something happened to her. It's better this way. She's safe."

"Oh, so you did it to *protect* her. Well, that makes all the difference in the world, doesn't it?"

"Sarah, knock it off," Karen said. "Amber's upstairs in our room watching television, and she doesn't need to hear this. Jessie's hurting too, in case you haven't noticed."

"Oh, I noticed," Sarah said tersely. "But at least Jessie knows the reason behind the hurt. Lynn walked out of here thinking she did something wrong." Sarah looked at Karen. "And I can't believe you went along with this."

"She tried to talk me out of it," Jessie said. "But she wants Lynn safe too." She'd thought Sarah would understand. The last thing any of them wanted was for Lynn to get hurt.

"Safe? Is that what you think?" Sarah asked. She stood and headed for the stairs. "Her heart's broken, Jessie. She was going to give up the life she's built in San Francisco in order to move up here and be with you. I think you hurt her a hell of a lot more than Wayne did. Her wrist will heal, but I'm not so sure about her heart."

Jessie was miserable. She'd known Wayne would find a way to screw things up for her. It really was inevitable.

"Maybe I should call her," Jessie said after Sarah had left.

"You did what you felt you had to do," Karen told her. "Wayne may only get a fine for violating the restraining order. His lawyer was slick enough to keep him from serving any time for putting you in the hospital. If he does end up spending time in jail for this, then you can tell her why you did what you did."

"Maybe I should have told her anyway. Sarah's probably right. Lynn should have had the opportunity to make the decision for herself."

"Jess, you can't beat yourself up over this. What's done is done. If he knows Lynn's gone, maybe he'll leave you alone as well. I want Lynn safe, but I want my sister safe even more."

Jessie hugged her arms tight around herself, praying that Karen was right, because at that moment, she was afraid she'd shatter into a million pieces.

CHAPTER TWENTY-SEVEN

L ynn managed to get in and out of her parents' house while they were away running errands. She took all of her things and left a note, knowing it was the coward's way out, but she couldn't face anybody. She was ready to head out of town when she decided to call Mike Williams. He'd come to their rescue the night before, and she wanted to catch up with him before getting the hell out of there.

He was waiting for her in a little coffee shop downtown and grinned broadly when she walked in. Lynn felt incredibly miserable about all that had happened, but his smile, as always, made her feel better. He stood and they embraced briefly before sitting.

"How have you been, Lynn?" he asked after the waitress came and took their orders. "You certainly look good. You haven't aged a bit in the past fifteen years."

"And you're still full of shit."

"It's really good to see you again. You said on the phone you're leaving. Any chance I could talk you into staying another day or two?"

"No, I've got to get back home."

"That's too bad. I'd have loved for you to meet Ryan. We've been together almost ten years now."

"Wow, Mikey, that's fantastic." Lynn squeezed his hand and smiled. There wasn't a better guy on earth as far as Lynn was concerned, and she was glad to hear he was happy.

"You have a better half waiting for you at home?"

"No." Lynn sighed, determined to change the subject. "I told the cop at the hospital last night who took my statement that I wanted to press charges against Wayne."

"I know. I talked to a friend at city hall. Unfortunately, he was only fined for the restraining-order violation. They let him out, but once his job in Nevada's done, he'll have a court date for your incident. Maybe he'll finally get some jail time."

"What do you mean? Wasn't he in jail after he put Jessie in the hospital?"

"Only for the few days it took to get him in front of a judge. He has a lawyer who knows his way around the system. Wayne was let off with a fine and spent little more than a weekend behind bars. It was a first offense, so they went easy on him."

Lynn looked out the window at the people passing by the coffee shop. Jessie had led her to believe Wayne had spent time in jail. Mike laid his hand on hers, and she shook her head with a sigh. "I can't believe she lied to me."

"Are you finally with Jessie? You seemed pretty close last night, and you've been in love with her forever, right? And you said there isn't anyone back home."

Lynn pulled her hand away and sat back from the table to allow the waitress space to set down their coffee. Mike had been one of her best friends in high school, and they'd told each other all their secrets. She'd been shocked when the quarterback of the football team had asked her to the homecoming dance, but less than an hour into their date, it all made sense. The rumors about Lynn being a lesbian were pretty well known, and she really didn't care what anyone thought about her.

But then Mike walked right up to her at lunchtime one day and asked her to the dance. At first she'd looked around, wondering if the cheerleaders were pulling some colossal joke on her, but he sat next to her in the cafeteria and convinced her he was serious. She'd agreed, and that was the beginning of a year-long relationship that stopped the rumors from circulating about her and kept them from starting about Mike.

Mike constantly pushed her to tell Jessie how she felt, and

Lynn pushed him to go after the love of his life, a popular drama student who'd starred in every production the school put on. Neither of them followed the other's advice, and instead spent their time together fantasizing about their respective love interests.

"We were together for about five seconds. After last night, she decided it was all a mistake."

"Ouch." Mike winced and took a sip of his coffee. "Maybe she'll change her mind? You know, just got scared?"

"That's what I thought last night." Lynn turned her attention to the people on the sidewalk again. "Trust me, Mikey, I still want to believe that, but after seeing her this morning, and now finding out that she lied to me about him doing jail time, I'm beginning to think she's right. Maybe I've held on to the fantasy for so damn long that it's finally warped my perception of reality."

"You know, Lynn, I was there the night he put her in the hospital. I got the call and was the first officer on scene. All she cared about, after making sure Amber was all right, was that no one tell you what happened. She was there on the floor, badly injured and waiting for the paramedics, and she made her family promise not to call you. She was scared to death that you'd hightail it up here and end up getting hurt, or even going to prison. She really cares about you, Lynn."

"I don't know what to do, Mike. I want…" Lynn glanced at the door and saw Wayne walking in with another man, laughing. She tried to keep her breathing even, but Mike must have seen the anger in her eyes, because he looked over his shoulder.

"Don't worry about him, Lynn." Mike moved his chair to try and block her view, but it was too late. Wayne had seen her and was walking toward their table. "Don't let him get to you."

"Lynn, I want to apologize for last night," Wayne said. He stopped next to her, and she refused to look at him, keeping her eyes on Mike.

"Get lost, Wayne. I don't want to talk to you."

"I understand how you feel."

Mike shook his head at her, but Lynn ignored his warning. She got to her feet and stood to face Wayne, who took a step back from her. "You will never understand how I feel, about *anything*." She spoke through clenched teeth, and the man with Wayne tried to pull him away. Lynn assumed he was his lawyer.

"I want to pay for your medical bills." Wayne motioned toward the cast on Lynn's arm. "It was my fault."

"Did you pay for Jessie's medical bills when you put her in the hospital?" Lynn saw a flash of rage cross Wayne's face and knew he'd love to get her away from other people.

"What goes on between me and Jessie is none of your business." He smiled to try and hide his fury. "Send your bills to my lawyer, and we'll see that they get paid."

"I don't want anything from you, you scumbag." Lynn pulled her arm away when Mike's hand tightened around her bicep. "Stay away from me, and stay away from Jessie. She wants you out of her life."

"Really? That's not what she told me when I talked to her a little while ago." He laughed, but he finally let his lawyer lead him away.

Lynn grabbed her keys and headed for the door, Mike at her heels. When they were outside, she whirled around and faced him. He ran into her before he could stop his forward motion.

"Do you have any idea how much I want to slug that bastard?"

"Lynn, he isn't worth it. Jessie would never forgive you."

"I need to get the hell out of this city." Lynn headed toward her car, but Mike grabbed her arm.

"You know he was only trying to rile you, right? You can't believe what he said."

"I don't know anything anymore." Lynn was so frustrated with the events of the past twenty-four hours that she wanted to cry. She wouldn't, though—not until she was well away from here and everyone she knew. "All I know is Jessie doesn't want me around anymore, so I'm going to give her what she wants. Please promise me you'll keep an eye on her and make sure she's okay."

"I will." Mike nodded and released his hold on her arm. "I have been, Lynn."

She started to walk away again but suddenly turned and threw her arms around his neck. He held her for a minute, and she kissed his cheek before pulling away.

"I'm sorry this wasn't a happier reunion." She forced a smile. "Thank you for being there last night, and thank you for being here for Jessie. You're a good friend, Mikey. I'll look you up when I come home next Christmas."

"I'll see you when you come back for his trial."

Lynn gritted her teeth. If she never saw Wayne Paulson again, it would be too soon.

CHAPTER TWENTY-EIGHT

S he still won't answer your calls?" Bri had been trying to get Lynn out of her funk for the entire week she'd been back in San Francisco. She was still mentally kicking herself for not sticking around long enough to get the true story out of someone— Jessie, Karen, Sarah—it really didn't matter who. Now that she was so far away, the fact that she'd run without putting up a fight was eating her up.

"She wanted to talk to me the morning after it happened. I basically told her I didn't understand why she was doing what she was doing, and I walked out." Lynn bent forward on the couch and held her head in her hands. She'd called her mother when she was only an hour away from Portland, and Rose had tried to get her to stay a few extra days, but at the time, Lynn only wanted to lick her wounds in private. "I only stayed long enough to press charges against that asshole, and then I came right back here. Well, after I had that confrontation with the prick."

"Any idea how long until the trial?"

"No, but they said someone would call me. I'll have to drive up for that, but otherwise, I guess I'm here for good."

Lynn was in a state of limbo. She'd phoned Jessie a thousand times since coming home seven days earlier, and her calls always went right to voice mail. She'd even tried Karen and Sarah, with the same result. Her mother hadn't heard from Jessie, but was encouraging her to keep trying. Bri was pushing her to move on.

It was becoming apparent that Jessie didn't want to talk to her, and what was she supposed to do, other than take Jessie's reasoning at face value?

"Are you coming out with me tonight?" Bri asked. She stood and looked down at Lynn. "Or do you intend to sit here and wallow in self-pity, and probably get drunk anyway?"

Lynn took a deep breath and looked at the phone, willing Jessie to call her back. If things had gone according to plan, she would have been on her way back to Portland to begin the rest of her life with Jessie.

"She'll leave a message if she wants to get in touch," Bri said.

Lynn looked at her. If Jessie didn't want her, maybe it was time to find someone who did. Just the thought made it feel as though her soul was being ripped apart, but what could she do? Jessie couldn't make her disinterest any more obvious than she already had. Lynn rubbed angrily at a tear on her cheek.

"No, no, no," Bri said, sitting again and putting an arm around Lynn's shoulders. Lynn tried to pull away, but Bri held tight. After a moment, Lynn finally sagged against her. "Lynn Patrick doesn't cry. I can't stand to see you like this, honey."

Lynn let the tears come unfettered. She hated feeling weak, and she abhorred crying, especially in front of other people. After a few moments she pulled away and stood, taking a deep breath and drying her eyes with the hem of her shirt.

"Can you wait for me to change?' she asked, actually managing to sound as if her heart wasn't breaking in two.

Jessie stared at the cell phone on the coffee table in front of her. She wanted Lynn to come back. Wayne had been let out with only a fine, and his lawyer had assured her he'd gone back to Vegas to finish his job there. That didn't stop Jessie from jumping every time the doorbell rang or a car door slammed.

"You're going to have to talk to her sooner or later," Sarah said from the kitchen doorway. Sarah was still angry at her for the way she had treated Lynn, but she still let Jessie and Amber stay with them, and Jessie loved her for it.

"It doesn't have to be today."

"You said that yesterday. And I'm sure you'll say it again tomorrow." Sarah sat next to her on the couch. "The more time you let go by without coming clean, the harder it'll be, Jess. It's only been a week since she left. You're making a huge mistake."

"Do you think she'll find someone else?" The possibility that she had pushed Lynn into the arms of another woman made Jessie nauseous.

"Honestly? It wouldn't surprise me if she did. I've never known Lynn to sit around and wallow in self-pity. *You* sent her away, Jess. *You* told her that you couldn't give her what she wanted. What's she supposed to do? She's loved you since you were kids. And you threw that back in her face without an explanation."

Jessie angrily swiped at a tear that was making its way down her cheek. She felt like she'd been crying for seven days straight. Given a choice, Lynn would choose to be by her side, and that was exactly why Jessie had done what she thought was right—to protect Lynn. But as she sat there staring at her cell phone, she couldn't think about anything except how much she loved Lynn. She wanted Lynn there to help her be strong, because she wasn't sure if she could deal with Wayne on her own any longer. And not only that. She wanted Lynn to share the good things too, the things that had less meaning now that she wasn't there.

Without giving herself time to change her mind, she grabbed the phone and flipped it open. Dialing Lynn's number, she took a deep breath, but her heart sank when, after five rings, it went to voice mail.

"Hi, Lynn…I'm sorry. I really don't know what else to say. Lynn, I love you. You were right—I sent you away because I was afraid Wayne would do something worse than break your wrist the next time. He told me that night he'd kill you if he ever saw us together again. I didn't know what else to do. Please come back, Lynn…I need you. I miss you. I know I can't apologize enough for not giving you the opportunity to make this decision for yourself, but I love you. I said that already, didn't I? I want to say it again and again." Jessie let out a choked laugh and used a tissue to remove another tear. "Please forgive me. *Please* call me back. I know this is all my fault, but ever since you left, I feel like I'm missing a part of myself."

Jessie sat back against the couch, clutching the phone. It was up to Lynn now. Hopefully she could accept her apology. If not, Jessie didn't know what she'd do.

❖

"Shit, I forgot my cell phone." Lynn stopped and felt in all her pockets, but it wasn't there. She turned to go back the few blocks to her loft, but Bri grabbed her arm.

"Forget it, Lynn. Just come inside for a couple of drinks and forget about your troubles for a while. You wouldn't be able to hear it if it rings while you're in here anyway."

Lynn wanted to argue, but Bri was right. Besides, what were the chances Jessie would call at all, when she hadn't answered Lynn's messages all week? Lynn nodded in defeat and rolled her shoulders to release some of her tension.

"Well, look who finally managed to crawl out of her hole," Renee said when they walked up to the bar. She put a shot of whiskey and a beer in front of Lynn, who flipped her the bird. Renee laughed and poured a glass of wine for Bri.

"She's a bit touchy this evening," Bri explained.

"You think?" Renee asked before going to the other end of the bar to help another customer.

"So, does anyone here tickle your fancy?" Bri asked, glancing around the bar. Lynn was sitting with her back to the dance floor and her elbows on the bar.

"What the hell does that mean?" Lynn didn't bother to hide her annoyance. "Where exactly is your fancy, and how would one go about tickling it?"

"Jesus, lighten up." Bri tapped her on the shoulder and pointed toward the door. "How about that one?"

"Leave me the fuck alone, will you?" Lynn didn't even bother to look in the direction Bri indicated. "I'm here because you didn't want me drinking at home alone, and I am *not* looking to pick up anyone. But if I were, I'd have no problem doing it on my own, as you've been so quick to point out on numerous prior occasions."

"Well, excuse me," Bri said with visible frustration. Without another word, she picked up her drink and headed for the opposite end of the bar.

Lynn spent the next few minutes peeling the label off her beer bottle and feeling sorry for herself. She was seriously considering going home when she felt a hand on her shoulder. She turned to meet the eyes of the pretty young thing who'd tried to pick her up the night of the wet T-shirt contest. The night before she'd left to go to Portland. To see Jessie. Damn it, she really needed to stop thinking about her.

"Excuse me," she said with a shy smile. "You're Lynn, right? God, I hope I remembered that correctly."

"Yeah, you did." Lynn forced a smile.

"Is anyone sitting here?" Lynn shook her head and motioned for her to have a seat. "You never called me. I guess I really didn't expect you to, but a part of me was hoping." She glanced down and noticed the cast on Lynn's arm for the first time. "Oh, my God, what happened?"

"It's just one of the hazards of being so desirable. But on the bright side, the cast makes it easier to fight off the women. You know, I lost your number." Lynn ran her good hand through her hair and scratched her temple. "I forgot your name too. That really isn't like me."

"Norah. You probably threw my number away."

"No, no, I didn't." She really hadn't, but she had absolutely no idea what she'd done with the napkin Norah had written it on. She motioned for Renee to get them another round and saw that Bri was giving her a thumbs-up. Lynn chose to ignore her. "You can even ask my friend over there."

"I'll take your word for it." Norah laughed, but she looked at Bri over Lynn's shoulder.

Lynn sighed quietly. It was way too easy. She wasn't even *trying* to pick up Norah. Lynn didn't object when Norah reached into her pocket for money to pay for their drinks.

"So, tell me, Lynn," Norah said when Renee walked away with her cash. "Are you in a better frame of mind tonight than you were the last time we met?"

"No," she answered honestly. She took a deep breath and met Norah's intense stare. "My frame of mind might be even worse than it was that night." Lynn didn't even think about what she was doing when she placed her good hand on Norah's thigh, right above her knee. Norah didn't seem to mind, so Lynn edged closer to her. "But I don't feel like going home alone tonight."

Norah glanced around nervously before redirecting her attention to Lynn. "I might be able to help you with that," she said with a slight smile.

Lynn was pleased to see the shy young woman she'd met that first night was still in there somewhere. She put her arm around Norah and kissed her on the cheek. "It's been a month since I met you. Don't tell me you still haven't been with a woman."

"I haven't." Norah's tone was a little too defensive. "I've only been here a couple of times since then. It's not like I come in here every night looking for someone."

"Hey, relax. I'm not judging you." Lynn stood and moved so her body was close to Norah's and her mouth was about an inch from Norah's ear. "I feel privileged that you want me to be your first. Someday you'll be in my shoes, Norah, and you'll understand what an incredible turn-on that is."

It was almost as though she flipped some kind of switch in Norah, who kissed her awkwardly.

When Lynn felt a hand groping between her legs, she pushed Norah away gently. "Slow down, honey," she told her with a chuckle. "The night's still young. Believe me—there's plenty of time for all that."

"I'm sorry."

Lynn saw the blush creeping up Norah's neck before she turned away. "Never be sorry for going after something you want."

An image of Jessie flashed in her head when she said those words. Jesus, why couldn't she stop thinking about her? Lynn took her seat once again and downed her second shot of whiskey before taking a swig of beer. "I need to tell you something before this goes any further."

"You have a girlfriend?"

"No," she answered bitterly, her thoughts again turning to Jessie. She shook her head to try and clear it. "But there is someone I haven't gotten over. I'm in love with her, and I can't honestly say I'll ever be over her. I can't promise you anything beyond tonight. You need to understand that before I walk out of here with you."

"I'm okay with that."

Lynn looked at her, searching for some kind of sign that Norah really did understand. What else could she do but believe Norah was okay with the arrangement? As far as Lynn was concerned, she'd done her duty by letting Norah know up front where things stood. If Norah had a problem with that the next morning, it certainly wouldn't be Lynn's fault, would it?

"At the risk of making a horrible mistake, I'll take your word for it." Lynn finished her beer, then took Norah by the hand, leading her toward the door.

"I'll call you tomorrow," Bri told her as they walked past, but Lynn only waved at her over her shoulder. She should have felt like things were finally getting back to normal, but in the company of another woman, she felt her loss even more acutely. And she refused to let Bri or anyone else see the truth in her eyes.

CHAPTER TWENTY-NINE

I want your hands on me, Lynn," Norah said breathlessly the very second Lynn closed the door behind them. "I've wanted you ever since I first saw you."

"Tell me what you want." Lynn began to unbutton Norah's blouse. Her cast made it difficult, and Lynn chuckled at her own clumsiness, ignoring the queasy feeling in her stomach at the memory of Jessie's skin under her hands. She finally gave up and moved her good hand to the top of Norah's jeans. "I'm at a bit of a disadvantage here, honey. You're going to have to undress yourself."

Without a word, Norah finished what Lynn had started, then let her blouse fall to the floor before undoing her bra and her pants. Guilt washed over Lynn at the sight of Norah standing naked before her, and she suddenly felt numb. She didn't resist when Norah kissed her, but when Norah began to urge her toward the bed as she was pulling Lynn's shirt from her pants, Lynn stopped and backed away from her, shaking her head.

"I can't do this," she whispered.

"Yes, you can." Norah grabbed Lynn's hand and tried to pull her closer, but Lynn jerked away and turned to walk into the kitchen.

"I'm sorry," Lynn said. When she faced her, she saw that Norah had followed her and was still completely naked.

"Did I do something wrong?"

Norah looked hurt and Lynn wanted to laugh, but she couldn't. Instead, a single tear rolled down her cheek. "No," Lynn answered.

"I know it sounds idiotic, but it isn't you, it's me. You're beautiful, Norah, but I want to be with someone else. I'm so sorry."

Lynn eventually told her to stay and insisted Norah take the bed and she would sleep on the couch. Before they turned in, they had a couple of shots while Lynn told Norah all about Jessie. Standing by the big picture window, Lynn glanced over toward the bed. She loved her loft, but times like this begged for privacy instead of this open layout. After toying with the idea of waking Norah and sending her on her way, she finally decided to simply let her sleep since it was the middle of the night. Lynn redirected her attention to the view outside her window.

Suddenly it occurred to her that she'd never checked her messages last night. Lynn had been so focused on Norah and trying to let her down easy, she'd forgotten. When she opened her phone and saw the missed call, she quickly pushed the button. Her heart sped up when she saw Jessie's name, and she fumbled as she dialed her voice mail.

Jessie's words lifted a huge weight from her shoulders, and she fell into the chair and listened to the rest of the message, unable to stop grinning. When it was done, she listened to it again, knowing she was being foolish, but damn, it was good to hear Jessie's voice. She was out of breath when she finally disconnected and quickly dialed Bri's number.

"Do you have any idea what fucking time it is?" Bri mumbled.

Lynn didn't care. She felt like rushing outside and yelling with joy. "Yeah, it's almost one thirty, and what are you doing home anyway? You usually close the bar." Lynn laughed, but a thought suddenly occurred to her. "Oh, shit—you got lucky, didn't you? You aren't alone?"

"You get a gold star, honey." Lynn heard sheets rustling, then a muffled voice. "Why exactly are you calling me this late? You didn't go home alone either."

"It's a long story, but nothing happened, and she's sleeping in the bed while I've forced my poor cat to share the couch with me." Lynn took a deep breath. "Jessie called while we were out. She loves me. I'm leaving for Portland in the morning, Bri, and I'm not coming back. Do you still want my loft?"

"Wait a minute—you're moving to Portland?"

"Yes. Do you want the loft, or do I need to put it on the market?"

"Slow down."

Lynn heard Bri take a deep breath, and she smiled. "Do I need to give you time to wake up?"

"What makes you think I was asleep?"

"Well, if you were in the middle of something I'd hope you'd have ignored the phone."

"All right, fine, I was asleep. You've really decided to move to Oregon?" Bri sounded disappointed, but Lynn couldn't worry about someone else's feelings now. She just wanted to pack what she absolutely needed and get the hell out of Dodge. "Things won't be the same without you here. I'll miss you."

"I know, and I'll miss you too, Bri. You're a great friend to put up with all my shit. At least you won't have to take care of Oscar for me anymore. And you'll always be welcome, no matter where I am."

"You're taking the devil cat? Thank God." Bri chuckled. "He was actually starting to grow on me, you know?"

"I'm leaving in the morning, Bri. Do you want the loft or not?"

"Of course I do. We'll work out the particulars later. Just go do what you have to do."

"Thanks, Bri. I love you."

"You too."

Lynn closed her phone and ran her fingers through her hair. Norah came out of the bathroom fully dressed and sat on the edge of the bed facing her. Lynn had been so wrapped up in her renewed happiness, she hadn't even noticed when Norah got up.

"Did I hear you say you're moving to Portland?"

"Jessie called. I need to get back there as soon as I can."

"Is she okay? I mean her husband—"

"She's fine. She said she loves me, and I don't want to spend another minute away from her." Lynn set the phone down on her desk and rested her elbows on her knees. "Norah, I'm really sorry about last night."

"Don't be." She shrugged as if it didn't matter, but even in the dim light Lynn could see pain in her eyes. "It was bad timing. Maybe if we'd met two months ago, things would have turned out differently. I'm happy you're getting what you want, Lynn."

"Thanks." Lynn stood, and Norah did the same. It seemed perfectly natural to embrace Norah, and Lynn gave her a quick kiss on the cheek.

"I'll let myself out."

As soon as she was gone, Lynn took out three suitcases, which she started filling with clothes. Oscar sat on the bed staring at her as though she were crazy. She pointed at him and smiled.

"Just you wait, mister. You're coming with me this time." He blinked and yawned, obviously bored with her, but he got up and walked to a half-filled suitcase to check out what she was doing. "I know a little girl who's going to fall in love with you."

She laughed when he meowed, and then he curled up on top of the clothes she'd put in the bag. She let him stay there while she packed her laptop and everything else she needed in order to do her work. After grabbing some things from the kitchen—and a few beers for celebrating after she got there—she started hauling everything out to the car. Oscar was content to lounge on her pillow after she'd removed him from the suitcase, and he watched everything with typical feline disinterest. But when she started gathering his food and toys he suddenly seemed nervous.

"Come on, buddy," she said when he ran under the bed at the sight of the carrier she pulled out of the closet. She should probably sleep for a few more hours, but she wanted to get to Jessie as fast as she could. She'd have time to sleep later.

CHAPTER THIRTY

L ynn glanced at her watch on her way from the car to the porch at Karen and Sarah's house.

She'd driven most of the night, stopping only for gas and a quick two-hour nap in the car. When she'd rolled into her parents' house at four o'clock that afternoon she'd been exhausted. After talking to her mother about a few things she made some important phone calls, one of which was to Karen, so she could set her plans in motion. She'd crashed for a couple more hours then and hadn't even bothered to unpack the things she'd brought from California. She hadn't called Jessie, because she hoped to surprise her.

She took a deep breath before ringing the bell. It took forever for Sarah to open the door, but when she did, she smiled and pulled Lynn inside for a big hug.

"Jessie's upstairs putting Amber to bed," she whispered. "Karen and I are going to run out for a bit so you two can be alone."

Lynn smiled when Karen came from the kitchen, and Sarah quickly handed her a jacket, motioning for her to hurry up. "Everything's taken care of, Lynn," Karen told her after a quick hug. "She'll be so happy to see you."

"Not nearly as happy as I will be to see her." Lynn shut the door behind them and hung up her jacket, then decided to wait in the kitchen so Jessie wouldn't see her the second she came down the steps. Lynn was standing at the sink with her back to the doorway when she heard Jessie coming.

"I swear that kid is getting harder and harder to put down

every—" She stopped with a look of confusion when Lynn turned to face her.

"I got your message."

"You didn't call back. I thought maybe you'd gotten over me already."

"I'll never get over you, Jess," Lynn said, then put her arms around Jessie's waist and pulled her close. When Jessie slid her arms around Lynn's neck to hold her, Lynn moved her mouth to Jessie's ear. "God, I've missed you."

"I'm so sorry." Jessie sobbed, and Lynn held her closer. "I was so afraid you'd never want to see me again."

"Hey," Lynn said, pulling back so she could meet Jessie's eyes. "I love you, Jess, and nothing will ever change how I feel. I spent almost twelve hours locked in a car with a screaming cat, so I hope to hell you don't tell me you changed your mind."

"No." Jessie laughed again and ignored her tears. "It almost killed me to be apart from you. Now that you're here, I don't intend to let you go ever again."

"Good. Now that we've settled that…" Lynn kissed her, and Jessie's tongue immediately tried to enter her mouth. Lynn obliged, moaning, and didn't pull away until she became dizzy from the lack of oxygen. "Wow."

"I missed you too."

"I can tell," Lynn answered with a grin. Jessie reached for her hand, but stepped away when she touched the cast.

"He's back in Vegas," Jessie said, taking a seat at the kitchen table.

"I know. I got a call from the courts this afternoon letting me know I need to be present for his hearing in ten days." Lynn sat next to her, wondering how to bring up what she wanted to propose. Jessie would most likely balk at the notion of being separated from Amber, even for a few days, especially since Amber had been with her grandmother for two weeks in December.

"I'm so sorry he did this to you, Lynn."

"I'm so sorry, Jess," Lynn said at the same moment. They both laughed, and some of the tension of the past two weeks dissipated.

"It's not the first argument he and I've had, and I'm sure it won't be the last," Jessie said after a moment. "I'm really glad you're here, Lynn, because you and I need to talk about some things."

Lynn didn't say a word, but simply poured them each a cup of coffee from the carafe that sat in the center of the table.

"I talked to Karen earlier this evening, and she told me about your conversation a few weeks ago." Jessie didn't look at Lynn while she spoke, but busied herself by putting some sugar into her coffee. "Between her and Sarah, I know what some of your fears are. I need to tell you about some of mine."

"Okay." Lynn's hands were trembling, and she tried not to let it show as she poured cream into her cup. The rest of her life depended on how their conversation went.

"You said you're in love with me, Lynn, but have you really thought about what that entails? I have a six-year-old daughter who demands a lot of my time." Jessie finally turned to meet Lynn's gaze, and Lynn sucked in a breath at the uncertainty in those brown eyes. "What exactly do you want to happen between us? I know what I want now, after almost losing you, but what do *you* want?"

"To help you raise your daughter. To be there for dance recitals, or baseball games, or whatever else she might end up showing an interest in." As Lynn spoke from her heart, the apprehension in Jessie's eyes began to fade. "I want to be there when she's sick and when she comes home crying from a scraped knee. I want to be there for you, Jess. I do love you, and I want what everyone wants— someone to share my life with. I want to sit with you on our back porch when we're seventy and hold your hand while we watch the sunset."

Lynn held her breath, half expecting Jessie to laugh. Jessie just watched her, and when she began to smile, Lynn relaxed. While she hadn't expected that particular question, it was far easier to answer than she would have thought. And she meant every word.

"Wow. I didn't expect that answer."

Jessie didn't pull away when Lynn covered her hand with one of her own, and Lynn sighed in relief. "I think you and I need some time alone. Away from here, and away from Wayne. Some place where he'll never even think to look for you."

"I can't go anywhere. Amber has school, and—"

"I've arranged everything." Lynn took Jessie's hand and raised it to her lips. She closed her eyes, still not quite believing that twenty-four hours ago she'd been close to making the worst mistake of her life with another woman. "Karen's going to take Amber to school in the mornings, and my mother will pick her up in the afternoons. We'll only be gone for a few days, Jessie."

"You've arranged all this with Karen?"

"I called her from my mom and dad's house this afternoon to work it all out."

"Where exactly do you want to take me for a few days?" Jessie's tone was skeptical, but Lynn could tell by the look in her eye that she would agree to go.

"Apparently my father bought a house at the coast for their fortieth anniversary. They'll be retiring in another few years, and they intend to move to Seaside when they do." Her parents had insisted she and Jessie go there for a few days to spend some time alone—and to talk about their future. "I want to take you there."

"I don't know what to say. I can't believe you managed to arrange all this so quickly."

"We have an incredible extended family that's willing to help us out. Will you go away with me?"

"Yes." Jessie caressed Lynn's cheek. "Yes. I'll go anywhere you want to take me. When do we leave?"

"As soon as Karen and Sarah get back. I have everything I need in the car, and all you have to do is pack a bag." Lynn stood and pulled her car keys out of her pocket. "I thought I'd leave Oscar here so he and Amber can get acquainted."

"Your screaming cat?" Jessie raised an eyebrow and got to her feet. "Is he good with kids?"

"I honestly don't know." Lynn laughed as she pulled Jessie into an embrace. "He's never been around them, but he puts up with me and my mood swings, so I think they'll be just fine."

CHAPTER THIRTY-ONE

Jessie grinned during the majority of the drive to Seaside. She was certain her grin was becoming a permanent fixture on her face, and nothing could make her happier—especially after she'd convinced herself she'd never be happy again. Even kissing Amber good-bye before they set off hadn't dampened her spirits, especially since Lynn's cat had already made himself comfortable on Amber's bed. The only thing threatening her happiness at the moment was Lynn's brooding. Her body language told Jessie that something was bothering her.

"I need to talk to you about something else," Lynn finally said when they were only a few miles from Seaside.

"Okay—"

"It's not that bad, Jess. Don't sound so worried." Lynn hesitated, and her expression turned more serious. "At least I hope it's not that bad."

Jessie stayed silent, waiting for her to speak again. Was it possible Lynn would take her all the way to the coast only to break up with her? Jessie tried to push that thought from her mind. When she'd shown up at Karen's unexpectedly she certainly hadn't acted like someone who wanted to end things. Unable to bear the quiet any longer, Jessie was about to say something when Lynn finally spoke again.

"I met Mike for a cup of coffee the morning I left to go back to San Francisco." Jessie looked at Lynn, who was staring straight ahead through the windshield, and thought she knew where the conversation was going. "Wayne showed up there with his lawyer and apologized for breaking my wrist." Lynn laughed, but continued to stare at the road before them. "He even offered to take care of my medical expenses."

"That was big of him." Jessie waited for the other shoe to drop. She should have been honest with Lynn about everything from the beginning.

"I called him a scumbag. I also told him to leave you alone. He implied he'd spoken to you and that wasn't what you wanted."

"What a bastard." Jessie put her hand on Lynn's thigh, and when Lynn glanced at her, Jessie tried to calm herself. If Wayne had been sitting next to her, she'd have punched him. "Baby, you know that's a lie, don't you? I have no desire to see or speak with him. Ever."

"I do know that." Lynn briefly held Jessie's hand before putting her good hand back on the steering wheel. "But at the time, you'd just sent me packing. Mike also told me Wayne never spent any time in jail for what he did to you, when you'd led me to believe that he did. Everything coalesced in my mind to make me think our separation was for the best."

"And when I was with Rick, it scared you. And you're still a little worried that I'll eventually go back to men. Am I right?" The look in Lynn's eyes told her everything she needed to know.

When Lynn nodded, Jessie turned in her seat to fully face her. "Listen to me. It would certainly be easier to stay with men. I've seen all the shit that Karen's had to go through. But you have to trust me when I tell you I've thought about this for quite some time. I didn't wake up one morning and think, 'Gee, it might be fun to be a lesbian today.' But then there's Wayne. You have to understand that I've been reluctant about this because of him. He threatened me, Lynn. He had to have known I'd been thinking about you. He told me if he ever found out I was with a woman, he'd kill me. Which, oddly, means he must have known that it was possible before I did. And then he threatened to kill you."

"If he ever comes near you, I'll kill him myself, Jessie."

When Jessie looked away, a tear ran down her cheek. She'd known Lynn would react that way, but was hoping she'd have said something else. She took a deep breath and refocused on Lynn.

"It scares me when you talk like that. I grew up with an abusive father, and now I'm divorcing an abusive husband. I don't want any more violence in my life. Jesus, I've wished him dead a time or two myself, but if it were to actually happen...I'd feel bad for having wished it."

"I'm sorry, Jess. I say things without thinking sometimes. It's just a figure of speech. The first time I was ever in a fight was with your father. The only other time was with Wayne on New Year's Eve. Neither one was much of a fight, though, was it?" Lynn gave a self-deprecating laugh, and Jessie couldn't help but smile. "I hate the thought of anyone hurting you, and I'd do whatever I had to in order to stop it. But you have to know I'm not a violent person, and I'd never raise a hand to you or to Amber. It might kill me if I ever hurt you like that. You mean so much to me, Jessie."

The plea in Lynn's eyes undid Jessie. She brought Lynn's hand to her lips and lightly brushed them across her knuckles.

"I do know that, Lynn, and I could never tell you how much you mean to me. You've always been here for me, and I'm sorry I didn't tell you when I was in the hospital. I'm sorry I asked your mother not to let you know too. And I'm sorry I lied about why I sent you away. I was trying to protect you, but I did it the wrong way," she said after a moment. She really didn't know what else to say. No words could excuse her lies.

"I think I understand why you did it, Jess." Lynn's voice was quiet, and Jessie inched closer so she could hear her. "I was angry at first, and then I was hurt. As the days went by, though, I began to understand. You were worried I'd do something stupid. I'd have lied to me too, if I'd been in your position."

"I'll never do it again, Lynn. I don't know what I'd do without you."

"I need to be honest with you about something too." Lynn glanced at her before turning into the driveway of the house. "Ten hours is a long time to be alone with yourself in the car. It tends to make you rather introspective. I found out a few things about myself on that trip to Frisco."

"Is this something I don't want to hear?" Jessie couldn't keep the trepidation from her voice, no matter how hard she tried. Lynn laughed, and she felt a little better.

"You can answer that for yourself when I'm done talking, deal?" Jessie nodded, and Lynn pulled Jessie's hand into her lap. She stared down at their entwined fingers as she spoke. "The woman you are now isn't the same woman I fell in love with so many years ago. I started to question whether I really loved you or if I was just in love with the fantasy of the way you used to be. I mean, you have a kid. Am I really ready for us to be a family?"

Lynn fell silent and continued staring at their hands, and Jessie was afraid she'd have a stroke. She waited for her to continue. Was it possible she hadn't truly meant what she'd said earlier about wanting to be there for both of them? *Jesus, Lynn, you're holding my entire life in your hands right now.*

"What did you conclude?" Jessie finally managed to ask. Lynn looked up at her then, and Jessie's breath caught in her throat. The pure love in Lynn's expression was unmistakable. Jessie caressed Lynn's cheek.

"That the reality of you is far better than the fantasy ever could have been. I love Amber. And I love her mother so much more than the girl I grew up with." Lynn smiled and melted into Jessie's touch. "I meant everything I told you before, Jess. I *am* ready to be a parent to Amber, if that's what you want from me."

"That is most definitely what I want." Jessie moved so they were closer, and she touched her lips to Lynn's briefly. It wasn't nearly enough, though, and Lynn kissed her again. Jessie put all of her feelings into that kiss, and when Lynn pulled away, breathing heavily, Jessie grinned. "I'm so happy right now."

Lynn pulled away from her. "So am I, but there's more." Lynn had decided the night before she'd never tell Jessie about Norah, but for some reason she needed to confess everything to her. Jessie's look of uncertainty made her falter, but she wanted to get it over with so they could let go of the past. "I told you about my friend Bri, right?"

"Yes."

"I went out to a bar with her last night, and she suggested that I stop moping around about you. I ran into a woman I'd met before and ended up taking her home with me." Lynn stopped to take a breath, and she risked meeting Jessie's eyes. The love she saw there was unwavering, and Lynn drew the strength she needed from it to go on. "I couldn't go through with it, Jessie. All I could think about was you. We spent over an hour talking about you and how much I'm in love."

"You didn't need to tell me about it." Jessie shook her head as she spoke, and Lynn felt a lot lighter. "Why did you?"

"Because I want us to be totally honest. I need you to know that I've grown up. That was something I learned about myself on the drive *back* to Portland. As much as I wished for us to be together over the past years, I really don't think it would have worked out. Everything that's happened in my life has brought me to this point— to be here with you now—and I don't want anything to ever come between us."

It felt like an eternity before Jessie finally spoke. "I love you," she said, then kissed her once again. "I knew you might find someone else if I sent you away. I'm glad to hear it didn't happen, even though you came close. Thank you for telling me."

"I'll never keep anything from you, Jess. You mean too much to me." Now that Lynn had said everything she needed to, she began to feel the effects of having been awake for the better part of the last thirty-six hours. "We should go inside before I fall asleep right here."

"You go to bed and I'll take our things inside."

"You're an angel." Lynn kissed her quickly and headed inside. Their lives would be perfect if Wayne would simply disappear forever.

CHAPTER THIRTY-TWO

L ynn walked into the kitchen the next morning and smiled contentedly when she saw Jessie standing at the stove making their breakfast. Lynn had been so tired when they'd finally arrived at the house the previous evening, she'd fallen asleep before Jessie finished bringing their bags in. As much as she'd wanted to make love, if she'd started anything, she'd have fallen asleep in the middle of it, and she definitely didn't want that to happen. She'd awakened alone and showered quickly before going to the kitchen.

"Good morning." Lynn walked up behind Jessie, put her arms around her, and pulled her back into her. Lynn didn't object when Jessie took hold of her hand and moved it up to cover her breast. "You have no idea how sorry I am for falling asleep on you last night. I was so looking forward to what you had planned when you finally got me alone."

"Breakfast can wait." Jessie switched off the stove and turned in Lynn's arms. "We didn't go to the store, so we don't have much anyway. I was about to heat a can of soup you had with your kitchen stuff. Good thing you didn't bother to unload at your parents."

"Did you check the date on the can?" Lynn wrinkled her nose. "I haven't bought soup in about three years."

Jessie laughed. "Then why did you bring it?"

"Honestly, I wasn't really paying much attention to what I was throwing in those bags. All I could think about was getting back to Portland." Lynn moved her hands to Jessie's butt and pulled her closer. She moved to kiss her, but stopped millimeters from Jessie's lips. "What do you say we go back to the bedroom for a little exercise, then I'll go to the store and buy us enough food to last a week?"

"I say yes." Jessie closed the remaining distance, but pulled away with a grin when Lynn tried to put her tongue into her mouth. Lynn moaned at the loss of heat, but Jessie took her hand and led her down the hall to the bedroom.

❖

Lynn opened her eyes a couple of hours later and moaned when she felt Jessie almost glued to her back. Jessie's hand was on her breast, her fingers teasing her nipple, and Lynn covered it to stop the movement.

"You wear me out," Lynn said. She sighed and allowed her eyes to close again. "It's a very nice feeling."

"Sorry, but I can't seem to get enough of you." Jessie's mouth was on the back of her neck, and Lynn moved away so she could turn over to face her.

"I don't recall saying it's a problem." Lynn pushed a stray lock of hair out of Jessie's eyes. "I guess I'll just have to be tired for the rest of my life. I could probably live with that."

"I love you, Lynn." Jessie's expression turned serious, and Lynn was worried about what she was about to say.

"Baby, what's wrong?"

"After Wayne did what he did to me," Jessie paused, and it was apparent she was trying hard to not cry, "I honestly didn't think I'd ever want to love anyone again. But I do. You have no idea how much it killed me to say I didn't want to be with you."

"Jess, it's okay." Lynn urged her closer and held her while Jessie pulled herself together. After a moment, Jessie backed away and wiped at her tears. "Okay, I can see I need to set up a ground rule here. I'd rather not talk about Wayne at all, but since he's the father of your child, that probably isn't feasible. So, my rule is—no talking about him while we're in bed. It's kind of creepy."

Jessie laughed, and Lynn kissed the tip of her nose. "Deal." Jessie sat up and rested against the headboard.

Lynn didn't object when Jessie encouraged her to lay her head in her lap. She closed her eyes and enjoyed Jessie's touch as Jessie threaded her fingers through her hair. "Can I ask you something?"

"Anything, baby." Lynn sighed with contentment and made herself comfortable.

"You told me you've always been in love with me. When exactly did you know?"

"I was seven."

"I'm serious." Jessie slapped her playfully on the shoulder.

"So am I. This family moved in across the street from us right before my birthday that year. They had a little girl my age, and my parents made me invite her to the skating party they'd planned for me at Oaks Park. I *really* didn't want to invite her. God, I didn't even know her. She didn't have any friends at school, and I'd never spoken to her before. My friends and I were going to have fun roller skating and riding rides, and I didn't want to have to worry about the new girl, but they forced me to include her.

"Anyway, we were at Oaks Park, and my favorite ride was always the Haunted House. My dad made me ride in the same car with the new girl, and I protested, but do you think he'd listen to me? About halfway through the ride, she got really scared, put her arms around my neck, and screamed right into my ear. Then she buried her face in my neck. She stole my heart and never gave it back." Lynn resituated herself so she could look into Jessie's eyes and smiled as she lightly ran her fingers along Jessie's cheek. "That was twenty-six years ago. And until last month, I couldn't get the courage to tell her how I felt."

"She feels the same way." Jessie took hold of Lynn's fingers, bringing them to her lips. "Trust me."

"I trust you with my life."

"I want to begin every day in your arms like this, Lynn."

Lynn quickly rolled onto her back and, with her good arm around Jessie, pulled her on top of her.

"How about if we start now?" Lynn moved her hand behind Jessie's neck and pulled her close for a kiss. When Jessie's hips pressed against her, Lynn wrapped her legs around Jessie's waist and held her in place. "God, Jessie. You feel so damn good."

"I need to be inside you, Lynn," Jessie whispered into her ear. Lynn allowed her legs to relax and moaned while Jessie kissed and licked her way down Lynn's neck. "You're so sexy. I love the way you react to my touch."

"I love the way you make me feel." Lynn arched into Jessie when her mouth closed around a nipple. "You make me feel so much."

She lost herself in Jessie's loving touch. Jessie's fingers were between her legs, stroking her slowly—torturously. Lynn's breathing quickened when Jessie teased her opening, and she groaned her disappointment when Jessie moved away.

"So impatient," Jessie murmured.

Lynn was grateful that Jessie seemed to be of the same mind. She held her breath when Jessie entered her, filling her more fully than she'd thought possible. Jessie pulled her fingers almost all the way out before thrusting them back in again. Lynn thrust beneath her, matching her movements and holding on tight to her when Jessie tried to navigate down between her legs.

"Stay here," she whispered, wrapping her legs around Jessie again, opening herself even more and causing the heel of Jessie's palm to press against her clit with each thrust. "Oh, Jess, so good, baby. I'm gonna come."

"Let it go, Lynn," Jessie said, breathing in gasps. "I want to feel you come with me inside you."

Lynn was afraid she might combust when the first twinges of orgasm began low in her belly. She thrust harder against Jessie's hand and pressed her head back into the pillow. The moment Jessie's teeth grazed the underside of her chin, Lynn arched her body and cried out as a ball of fire exploded between her legs and her orgasm ripped through her body.

An eternity seemed to pass before the humming throughout her body receded. Jessie slowly removed her fingers, and Lynn whimpered at the void left behind. "I think I've died and gone to heaven," she managed in a raspy voice. She couldn't seem to open her eyes, but she didn't care. She felt something she'd never felt before—satisfaction. The bed moved, and she grabbed Jessie's hand. "Where do you think you're going? I'm not anywhere near finished with you."

"I certainly hope not." Jessie chuckled. "I just needed to catch my breath. I can't keep my hands off you, and that makes it difficult to calm myself."

"What makes you think I want you calm?" Lynn grinned and finally managed to open her eyes. "I kind of like you breathless."

Jessie laughed, but then moaned when Lynn slid her hand slowly down Jessie's torso. The cast kept her from doing everything she wanted, but she quickly nestled between Jessie's legs. The heady scent of Jessie's arousal made her light-headed. Lynn closed her eyes and breathed deeply.

"Damn, you're so beautifully sexy," Lynn murmured with reverence before taking Jessie's clit between her lips. She eased off when Jessie threaded her fingers through Lynn's hair, something Lynn was quickly beginning to realize meant she was close to coming. At Jessie's whimpered protest, Lynn entered her with her tongue, reveling in the wetness that coated her face.

"Please don't tease me, Lynn." Jessie's breaths were ragged with need. "I need you so bad."

"I'm right here, baby." Lynn ran her tongue the length of Jessie's sex, eliciting a groan that made Lynn instantly hard and ready again. "Ah, fuck, the things you do to me, Jess."

"You do some pretty incred...oh, yeah." Jessie went rigid beneath her when Lynn took her clit in her mouth again. Jessie held her tight to her body as she came hard all over her face. Lynn didn't stop her insistent sucking and licking until Jessie went limp and had to push her away. "Stop...fuck...I think you've wrecked me."

"I hope not." Lynn kissed her way back up to Jessie's lips, taking a moment to pay particular attention to each tantalizing breast along the way. "I have plans for you that run an entire lifetime, not just this morning."

"Good to know." Jessie laughed but the sound came out weakly. She managed to get her arms around Lynn and pulled her up on top of her. "I wish someone had told me sex could always be this incredibly mind-blowing."

"I love you so much, Jess." Lynn couldn't hold herself up on her broken wrist any longer, and she rolled off onto her back.

"I love you too." Jessie curled up against her, one hand moving lazily across Lynn's abdomen. "More than I ever thought possible."

❖

Lynn had her head pressed into the pillow with her eyes closed when Jessie's hand suddenly stopped its motion, her body going rigid. Lynn's eyes flew open.

"Did you hear that?" Jessie asked.

"Fuck, the only thing I can hear is the pulse roaring in my ears."

"I'm serious, Lynn." Jessie pushed off her and sat on the edge of the bed, her attention drawn to the doorway.

"What was it?" Lynn jumped out of bed and quickly pulled on her sweatpants and a shirt before going to sit next to Jessie. Jessie was obviously spooked, and although Lynn hadn't heard any noises, it was apparent Jessie had.

"It sounded like glass breaking." Jessie grabbed Lynn's hand when she stood to check things out. "What are you doing?"

"I'm going to go see what it was." Jessie shook her head and refused to let go of Lynn's hand. Lynn knelt down in front of her. She could tell from the fear in Jessie's eyes exactly what she was thinking. "Baby, there's absolutely no way he could know about this house. My dad just closed on it last month. A cat or raccoon or something probably knocked one of those flowerpots off the railing on the front porch. Just let me go check. I'll be right back."

"Lynn, if he ever caught us together like this," Jessie indicated the disheveled bed and her lack of clothing, "he'd kill us both."

"He won't find us like this. I'm hoping he'll go to jail for this."

Lynn raised her cast. "If luck's on our side, maybe he'll leave you alone after that." Lynn let Jessie hold her for a minute, then pulled away.

Jessie searched her face and glanced toward the door before she let go of Lynn's hand.

"Be careful, all right?"

"Stay right here." Even though the house had been completely quiet for the past few minutes, Jessie's fear had obviously affected her. Her heart was racing, and it had nothing to do with the activity they'd been about to engage in moments ago. She searched the house and saw no broken windows. The kitchen yielded no answers either, so Lynn opened the front door and saw a flowerpot in pieces on the porch, just as she'd predicted. She let out her held breath and chuckled at her own nervousness. She closed the door and went back to the bedroom. "It *was* a flowerpot."

"Are you sure?"

"Positive." Lynn held a hand out to Jessie and pulled her to her feet. "I'm going to take a quick shower, then head to the store for some groceries. Care to join me?"

"For the shower or the grocery trip?" Jessie gave a slight smile, but it was obviously forced. Lynn could tell she wasn't completely at ease yet.

"Either. Both." Lynn gave her a roguish grin. "Your choice."

CHAPTER THIRTY-THREE

Jessie had taken Lynn up on the offer of a joint shower, but decided to stay at the house while Lynn went to the grocery store. She was putting wood in the fireplace when she heard a knock at the door. She smiled and shook her head, because Lynn had left not five minutes earlier. She must have forgotten something. As Jessie neared the door, she hesitated, remembering the broken flowerpot from earlier. She wasn't totally convinced that an animal had knocked it to the ground.

"Who is it?" she asked, standing next to the door.

"Officer Mullins, Seaside Police, ma'am. Mike Williams from the Portland PD called and asked that we check on you."

Jessie eased aside the curtain covering the tall pane of glass next to the door and peered out. He was holding his badge up for her to see, and she was suddenly glad she and Lynn had someone like Mike to look out for them. She took a deep breath and opened the door.

"Sorry to bother you, ma'am," he said with a polite smile as he removed his hat. "Officer Williams seemed to think you might be in some danger."

"I'm sure he only wanted to make sure we got here okay," Jessie told him.

"No offense, ma'am, but if that were the case, why didn't he just call you?" The man was right, but Jessie wished he'd stop calling her *ma'am*. It made her feel old.

"We turned off our phones when we got here." Jessie shrugged apologetically before walking to the dining room and looking through her purse. "I must have left my cell in the car last night. I'll call Mike as soon as my girlfriend gets back and let him know we're okay."

"All right." For some reason, he seemed reluctant to leave. He put his hat back on and tilted his head at her. As if remembering something he'd forgotten, he looked at the small notebook in his hand. "Would you be Jessica Greenfield or Lynn Patrick? I need to make a note of who I spoke with."

"I'm Jessica."

"Very good, ma'am. You have a nice day."

Jessie shut the door and bolted it so she could return to the fireplace. She wanted to have a nice fire going when Lynn returned. She'd tossed the last of the kindling in and was about to light the match when she heard another knock at the door.

"Jesus, it's like Grand Central Station here tonight. Who is it?"

"Officer Mullins again, ma'am. Just one more thing."

She hesitated because the voice sounded different, but her fingers acted before her brain could engage, and as soon as she turned the deadbolt, the door crashed open, slamming into her and knocking her off balance.

Jessie had only a moment to realize who it was before Wayne grabbed her by the neck. As he sneered at her, he picked her up with one hand before he slammed her into the wall beside the door. He held her there by the throat, and Jessie was dimly aware that her feet weren't touching the ground.

"You fucking bitch," he said through clenched teeth.

Jessie was surprised that his breath didn't smell like alcohol. Thinking that he could do this without being drunk scared her even more. She tried to concentrate on breathing, which was difficult with his hand on her throat.

"You've made a fool out of me, and I've lost *two* jobs because of you now. I got fired because I had to spend the night in jail when that dyke broke her arm and I couldn't get back to Vegas on time. Why do you keep doing these things to me, Jessie?"

"Wayne," she managed to say between desperate gasps for air. "Amber—"

"Do you think I'm stupid? I know she's not here." His eyes darted around, and he seemed to be having trouble focusing on her. He might not have been drinking, but he was definitely high on something. He laughed and shook his head as he grinned wickedly. "I also know your girlfriend left ten minutes ago. We're all alone, Jessie, and believe me, I'll have plenty of time to finish what I came here for before she gets back."

He looked around the house but quickly returned his attention to her. The pressure on her windpipe was becoming unbearable, and she was afraid she might pass out—or worse.

"Police…" Jessie gasped. She began to claw at his arm. She'd been trying not to fight back, knowing that would only make him angrier, but as her air supply dwindled, her survival instincts kicked in.

"Don't you worry about Officer Mullins." Wayne laughed again as he pulled her away from the wall and slammed her back into it. Jessie saw little white floaters in her line of vision, and the room started to swim. Just when she was certain she could no longer fight the darkness that threatened, he dropped her to the floor without warning and strode toward the kitchen. "There's no chance in hell he'll be able to help you."

As Jessie rubbed her neck and struggled to breathe, she heard him open the refrigerator and take out one of the beers Lynn had brought with her from San Francisco. If Wayne intended to kill her, hopefully Lynn wouldn't walk in on him. In fact, if that's what happened, she hoped Wayne would be gone long before Lynn got back. She heard him twist the cap off the beer and toss it on the counter.

Jessie remembered her purse on the dining-room table. She crawled in that direction, pleading with whatever entity might be listening that Wayne would stay in the kitchen long enough for her to reach it. Her throat burned horribly, and she fought back tears. She refused to let him see any weakness in her. She'd almost reached her purse when a laugh came from behind her; then he grabbed her by the back of her shirt. He threw her over onto her back and straddled her, immobilizing her. For one horrendous moment, she was certain he intended to rape her.

Instead, he reached behind his back and pulled out a knife, its long blade covered in blood. Jessie's heart lurched, and when he smiled at her, she understood why he knew Officer Mullins would not be coming to her rescue.

❖

Lynn was on her way back to the house, still cursing herself for forgetting her wallet. She'd actually made it all the way to the store before realizing she didn't have it. She pulled out her cell phone and decided to listen to her messages on the drive back. She was just hitting the keys with her password when a call came in. It was Karen.

"Hey," Lynn said as she pulled out of the store's parking lot.

"Jesus Christ, where the fuck have you been?" Karen said, her tone frantic.

"We accidentally left our phones in the car last night."

"Please tell me you and Jessie are all right. Let me talk to her."

"I'm heading back to the house now. I'll have her—"

"Fuck! You aren't with her?"

"What's wrong with you, Karen?" She heard Karen speak to Sarah, and Lynn began to get perturbed. "What the hell's going on?"

"Wayne called me a little while ago."

"Jesus, is that all? You had me scared." Lynn felt relieved at Karen's words. "He has no idea where we are, and we're fine."

"Lynn, I didn't recognize the number, and when we hung up, I looked it up on the computer because he said he planned to end this once and for all. It was a Seaside number. He's there, Lynn. He must have followed you guys last night."

Lynn had never experienced such a level of panic. She suddenly remembered the flowerpot knocked over on the front porch and slammed her foot down on the gas pedal. She was aware of nothing but the road in front of her as she sped toward the house.

"I called Mike. He had someone from the police department there go out to the house." Karen's voice sounded as if it were a thousand miles away. Lynn swore to herself that if Wayne had touched Jessie, she really would kill him. "Sarah and I are on our way there, and so are your dad and my mom. And Mike is coming too."

Lynn didn't slow down until she'd turned the corner onto the street where the house was. Thank God the police cruiser was parked in the driveway, but no other cars were on the street.

"The cops are here," she told Karen. "I'll call back when I know Jessie is okay."

She tossed her phone aside and pulled in next to the cruiser. When she got out of the car, she saw the front door to the house wide open. She glanced at the cruiser warily, afraid of what she might find. The driver's side door was open and a hand was visible on the ground. She looked quickly around the street. How odd that there wasn't a crowd of people wanting to see why the cops were there. In San Francisco people would have been everywhere. But this was the Oregon coast in early January—not exactly the height of tourist season—and most of the locals were probably at work. Her legs were shaking as she forced herself to walk around to the other side of the cruiser.

"Jesus," she muttered just before she put her hand over her mouth. The cop was dead, blood everywhere from his slashed throat. His eyes were wide open, staring at nothing. Lynn bent forward, her hands on her knees, and willed herself not to throw up. After a few deep breaths with her eyes closed, she forced herself to move. Hopefully she wasn't too late to save Jessie.

CHAPTER THIRTY-FOUR

L ynn was breathing so fast, and her heart was beating so hard, she was almost certain she'd pass out before she even made it to the front door. She braced herself for the worst, but when she looked inside, she couldn't see anything wrong, other than the door itself, which looked like the hinges were about to give way. She cautiously crept inside, sticking close to the wall. A man's voice was coming from the dining room, and she cursed under her breath when she realized that Jessie's purse—and her gun—were on the table in there.

"You're going to die, and when your girlfriend comes back, I'll be waiting for her and kill her too." Lynn forced herself to breathe, and before she could think twice about what she was doing, she stepped into the dining room.

Jessie's eyes immediately went to her, and Lynn realized she'd made a mistake. Jessie's reflex action would alert him to her presence. Lynn was enraged. Wayne was on top of Jessie, with a knife to her throat—an extremely bloody knife. At first she thought he'd already hurt Jessie, but then she remembered the cop out front, and she managed to stop herself from gagging at the image that invaded her mind.

"Oh, how nice." When Wayne stretched back a bit to look at her, Lynn realized he had Jessie's arms immobilized. She began to struggle now that the knife wasn't pointed at her jugular vein. "We can start the party now."

"If you want to hurt somebody, come and get me," Lynn told

him, never taking her eyes from Jessie. Jessie's eyes were round with shock, and she shook her head frantically at Lynn, but Lynn kept on talking. "Leave Jessie alone, Wayne. It's really me you want, isn't it?"

"I want to kill you both, but I really don't care who goes first." He glanced down at Jessie, but didn't look away long enough for Lynn to make a move against him. "If you try anything stupid, I *will* make this slow and very painful for you both, do you understand me, bitch?"

Jessie nodded quickly before looking back at Lynn. She shook her head again, tears rolling down her cheeks. Lynn had to look away from her or she'd lose her resolve to do what she had to do.

"Let her go, Wayne. You can have me if you let her go."

"You don't get it, do you, you fucking cunt?" Lynn was surprised by his agility. He was on his feet and in her face before she knew what was happening. He grabbed the front of her shirt and shoved her against the wall. "This isn't an either/or situation, and neither one of you is going anywhere unless it's in a body bag."

Lynn forced herself to look in his eyes. She wished she'd thought to ask Karen how far away they were. She wished she'd told her parents she loved them before she and Jessie had left for Seaside. As images from her life began to flash before her eyes, she managed to focus on her fury the day Jessie's father hit her.

She stood up straight and took a deep breath. When he smiled and brought the knife back so he could plunge it into her chest, Lynn raised her arm to block it. The knife hit her cast, and he dropped it. At that same moment Lynn heard a roar, and Wayne's eyes went wide. He turned to look behind him, then crumpled to the ground. For a moment, Lynn stood completely still before she fully realized what had happened. Jessie dropped the gun and fell to her knees. Lynn's paralysis finally broke, and she ran to Jessie's side.

"Baby, are you all right?" she asked as Jessie clung to her. Jessie cried uncontrollably, her body shaking in time to her sobs. Lynn sat on the floor and held Jessie in her lap, rocking back and forth as Jessie's hands fisted her shirt.

"What the fuck were you thinking?" Jessie's voice sounded strained and hoarse. "He could have killed you, Lynn."

"He would have killed *you* if I hadn't stopped him, Jess," Lynn said. "If I'd been thinking, I'd have grabbed the cop's gun and shot Wayne before he ever saw me. All I could think about was getting in here to save you."

"Oh, my God." Jessie raised her head to look at her. "He really killed the cop, didn't he?"

"Yes, he did," someone behind them said. Lynn looked up to see Mike standing over Wayne's body.

"Is he dead?" Lynn indicated Wayne with a toss of her head. She didn't intend to let go of Jessie just yet. Mike knelt down and felt for a pulse, then nodded.

"Amber..." Jessie began to cry.

"Amber's fine, baby."

"I killed her father."

The horror in Jessie's eyes broke Lynn's heart. She held Jessie tighter and stroked her hair.

"Shhh," she murmured. "You did it to save your own life, Jess. And mine. She'll understand that when she's old enough to comprehend what really happened between you and him."

Lynn tried to stop her own tears from falling as Jessie sobbed in her arms. The relief at how things turned out hadn't yet kicked in, and she realized how close she'd come to losing Jessie forever. But it wasn't about her right then, and she wouldn't let Jessie see how scared she still was.

CHAPTER THIRTY-FIVE

Lynn opened the door for Jessie and helped her out of the car. They were home from Seaside and staying at Lynn's parents' home since her mother had driven to Seaside to help clean the house. Jessie had spent a couple of nights in the hospital, and the doctors released her that morning. The cursory decision on Wayne's death was self-defense, and according to Mike, the Seaside Police Department would concur, especially because Wayne had killed one of their officers. Wayne was really gone, and Jessie was having a hard time dealing with that fact.

"Thank you for bringing me home." Jessie's voice was still raspy since Wayne had almost crushed her windpipe. Lynn supported her with an arm around her shoulders.

"You don't have to thank me, baby," Lynn said quietly. "I'd rather be by your side than anywhere else."

"I want to shower and relax for a bit before Karen brings Amber over." Jessie headed up the steps as soon as they walked into the house.

"Do you need some help?"

"No. Maybe some coffee when I'm done?"

"You got it." Lynn went to the kitchen to start brewing the coffee. When she was done, she realized she hadn't heard any noise from upstairs, so she went up to check on Jessie. Jessie was sitting on her bed staring out the window. After a moment, Lynn sat next to her. Jessie rested her head on her shoulder without a word, and they sat without speaking.

"He's really gone," Jessie finally said with a sigh. Lynn didn't know how to respond, so she gently rubbed the small of Jessie's back. "I should feel bad, but I don't, Lynn. Don't get me wrong—I'm upset that I took another human being's life and that it was my daughter's father. But I don't feel bad that Wayne—our abuser—is dead. Does that make me a horrible person?"

"No, Jess, it doesn't." Lynn held her a little closer and pressed her lips to Jessie's temple. "He was a waste of space." Lynn cringed when she felt Jessie's shoulders shake. Christ, could she be any more insensitive? "I'm sorry, I—"

"Don't apologize."

"Are you laughing?" Lynn began to laugh softly too, and Jessie finally let it out.

"You're absolutely right—he *was* a waste of space." Jessie lay back on the bed and urged Lynn to lie next to her. "God, I don't know how I'm going to tell Amber."

"She doesn't need to know everything yet," Lynn said, closing her eyes as Jessie placed her head on Lynn's chest. "She just needs to know right now that her father's gone. You can explain it all to her when she's older."

"*We* can explain it all to her when she's older," Jessie said, giving Lynn a squeeze. "I want you to move in with us."

"Are you sure?" Lynn didn't want to push. Her heart was somersaulting with joy, but she wanted to be certain Jessie wanted it.

"Yes." Jessie propped herself up so she was looking down into Lynn's face. "I know what I want, Lynn. What do you want right now?"

"To be with you, now and forever." She caressed Jessie's cheek with the back of her fingers. "I wasn't sure you'd want to live together right away though."

"I don't want to waste another second being without you."

"In that house?"

"I love the house, and I love you. Wayne and I didn't live there together for very long. We only bought it a couple of years ago, and he hasn't been there for almost a year." Jessie traced Lynn's lips with a finger, and Lynn kissed the tip of it. "You and I can make memories there now."

"We'll have to get some deck chairs so we can sit outside and hold hands while we watch the sunset."

"Deal." Jessie said.

Lynn settled her head on Jessie's chest, loving the strong, steady sound of the heartbeat coming from within, because she knew they had come too close to having it silenced forever. She closed her eyes and held onto Jessie's hand, knowing that she was finally right where she belonged.

About the Author

PJ Trebelhorn was born and raised in the greater metropolitan area of Portland, Oregon. Her love of sports—mainly baseball and ice hockey—was fueled in part by her father's interests. She likes to brag about the fact that her uncle managed the Milwaukee Brewers for five years and the Chicago Cubs for one year.

PJ now resides in eastern Pennsylvania with Cheryl, her partner of many years, and their menagerie of pets—six cats and one very neurotic dog. When not writing or reading, PJ spends her time rooting for the Flyers, Phillies, and Eagles, or watching movies.

Books Available From Bold Strokes Books

True Confessions by PJ Trebelhorn. Lynn Patrick finally has a chance with the only woman she's ever loved, her lifelong friend Jessica Greenfield, but Jessie is still tormented by an abusive past. (978-1-60282-216-0)

Jane Doe by Lisa Girolami. On a getaway trip to Las Vegas, Emily Carver gambles on a chance for true love and discovers that sometimes in order to find yourself, you have to start from scratch. (978-1-60282-217-7)

Blood Hunt by LL Raand. In the second Midnight Hunters Novel, Detective Jody Gates, heir to a powerful Vampire clan, forges an uneasy alliance with Sylvan, the Wolf Were Alpha, to battle a shadow army of humans and rogue Weres, while fighting her growing hunger for human reporter Becca Land. (978-1-60282-209-2)

Loving Liz by Bobbi Marolt. When theater actor Marty Jamison turns diva and Liz Chandler walks out on her, Marty must confront a cheating lover from the past to understand why life is crumbling around her. (978-1-60282-210-8)

Kiss the Rain by Larkin Rose. How will successful fashion designer Eve Harris react when she discovers the new woman in her life, Jodi, and her secret fantasy phone date, Lexi, are one and the same? (978-1-60282-211-5)

Sarah, Son of God by Justine Saracen. In a story within a story within a story, a transgendered beauty takes us through Stonewall-rioting New York, Venice under the Inquisition, and Nero's Rome. (978-1-60282-212-2)

Sleeping Angel by Greg Herren. Eric Matthews survives a terrible car accident only to find out everyone in town thinks he's a murderer—and he has to clear his name even though he has no memories of what happened. (978-1-60282-214-6)

Dying to Live by Kim Baldwin & Xenia Alexiou. British socialite Zoe Anderson-Howe's pampered life is abruptly shattered when she's taken hostage by FARC guerrillas while on a business trip to Bogota, and Elite Operative Fetch must rescue her to complete her own harrowing mission. (978-1-60282-200-9)

Indigo Moon by Gill McKnight. Hope Glassy and Godfrey Meyers are on a mercy mission to save their friend Isabelle after she is attacked by a rogue werewolf—but does Isabelle want to be saved from the sexy wolf who claimed her as a mate? (978-1-60282-201-6)

Parties in Congress by Colette Moody. Bijal Rao, Indian-American moderate Independent, gets the break of her career when she's hired to work on the congressional campaign of Janet Denton—until she meets her remarkably attractive and charismatic opponent, Colleen O'Bannon. (978-1-60282-202-3)

Black Fire: Gay African-American Erotica, edited by Shane Allison. *Black Fire* celebrates the heat and power of sex between black men: the rude B-boys and gorgeous thugs, the worshippers of heavenly ass, and the devoutly religious in their forays through the subterranean grottoes of the down-low world. (978-1-60282-206-1)

The Collectors by Leslie Gowan. Laura owns what might be the world's most extensive collection of BDSM lesbian erotica, but that's as close as she's gotten to the world of her fantasies. Until, that is, her friend Adele introduces her to Adele's mistress Jeanne—art collector, heiress, and experienced dominant. With Jeanne's first command, Laura's life changes forever. (978-1-60282-208-5)

Breathless, edited by Radclyffe and Stacia Seaman. Bold Strokes Books romance authors give readers a glimpse into the lives of favorite couples celebrating special moments "after the honeymoon ends." Enjoy a new look at lesbians in love or revisit favorite characters from some of BSB's best-selling romances. (978-1-60282-207-8)

Breaker's Passion by Julie Cannon. Leaving a trail of broken hearts scattered across the Hawaiian Islands, surf instructor Colby Taylor is running full speed away from her selfish actions years earlier until she collides with Elizabeth Collins, a stuffy, judgmental college professor who changes everything. (978-1-60282-196-5)

Justifiable Risk by V.K. Powell. Work is the only thing that interests homicide detective Greer Ellis until internationally renowned journalist Eva Saldana comes to town looking for answers in her brother's death—then attraction threatens to override duty. (978-1-60282-197-2)

Nothing But the Truth by Carsen Taite. Sparks fly when two top-notch attorneys battle each other in the high-risk arena of the courtroom, but when a strange turn of events turns one of them from advocate to witness, prosecutor Ryan Foster and defense attorney Brett Logan join forces in their search for the truth. (978-1-60282-198-9)

Maye's Request by Clifford Henderson. When Brianna Bell promises her ailing mother she'll heal the rift between her "other two" parents, she discovers how little she knows about those closest to her and the impact family has on the fabric of our lives. (978-1-60282-199-6)

Chasing Love by Ronica Black. Adrian Edwards is looking for love—at girl bars, shady chat rooms, and women's sporting events—but love remains elusive until she looks closer to home. (978-1-60282-192-7)

Rum Spring by Yolanda Wallace. Rebecca Lapp is a devout follower of her Amish faith and a firm believer in the Ordnung, the set of rules that govern her life in the tiny Pennsylvania town she calls home. When she falls in love with a young "English" woman, however, the rules go out the window. (978-1-60282-193-4)

Indelible by Jove Belle. A single mother committed to shielding her son from the parade of transient relationships she endured as a child tries to resist the allure of a tattoo artist who already has a sometimes-girlfriend. (978-1-60282-194-1)

The Straight Shooter by Paul Faraday. With the help of his good pals Beso Tangelo and Jorge Ramirez, Nate Dainty tackles the Case of the Missing Porn Star, none other than his latest heartthrob—Myles Long! (978-1-60282-195-8)

Head Trip by D.L. Line. Shelby Hutchinson, a young computer professional, can't wait to take a virtual trip. She soon learns that chasing spies through Cold War Europe might be a great adventure, but nothing is ever as easy as it seems—especially love. (978-1-60282-187-3)

Desire by Starlight by Radclyffe. The only thing that might possibly save romance author Jenna Hardy from dying of boredom during a summer of forced R&R is a dalliance with Gardner Davis, the local vet—even if Gard is as unimpressed with Jenna's charms as she appears to be with Jenna's fame. (978-1-60282-188-0)

River Walker by Cate Culpepper. Grady Wrenn, a cultural anthropologist, and Elena Montalvo, a spiritual healer, must find a way to end the River Walker's murderous vendetta—and overcome a maze of cultural barriers to find each other. (978-1-60282-189-7)

Blood Sacraments, edited by Todd Gregory. In these tales of the gay vampire, some of today's top erotic writers explore the duality of blood lust coupled with passion and sensuality. (978-1-60282-190-3)

Mesmerized by David-Matthew Barnes. Through her close friendship with Brodie and Lance, Serena Albright learns about the many forms of love and finds comfort for the grief and guilt she feels over the brutal death of her older brother, the victim of a hate crime. (978-1-60282-191-0)

Whatever Gods May Be by Sophia Kell Hagin. Army sniper Jamie Gwynmorgan expects to fight hard for her country and her future. What she never expects is to find love. (978-1-60282-183-5)

nevermore by Nell Stark and Trinity Tam. In this sequel to *everafter*, Vampire Valentine Darrow and Were Alexa Newland confront a mysterious disease that ravages the shifter population of New York City. (978-1-60282-184-2)

Playing the Player by Lea Santos. Grace Obregon is beautiful, vulnerable, and exactly the kind of woman Madeira Pacias usually avoids, but when Madeira rescues Grace from a traffic accident, escape is impossible. (978-1-60282-185-9)